#CYBERPUNK**NOW**
AND THE DYSTOPIAN MOMENT

#CYBERPUNK**NOW**

AND THE DYSTOPIAN MOMENT

LR

The London Reader

Volume One

www.LondonReader.uk

The London Reader
Contemporary Voices in Creative Writing

Find the London Reader online:
www.LondonReader.uk
www.patreon.com/LondonReader
www.amazon.co.uk/The-London-Reader/dp/B01L7J8P4A
www.amazon.com/The-London-Reader/dp/B01L7J8P4A
www.facebook.com/LondonReaderMag
www.twitter.com/LondonReaderMag

The London Reader, Volume 1, #cyberpunkNOW and the Dystopian Moment
Abridged edition first released to subscribers in Autumn 2016.
© The London Reader, 2020
All rights reserved.
ISBN-13: 978-1-989633-00-7 (print)
ISBN-13: 978-1-989633-01-4 (electronic)

The cover image of #cyberpunkNOW has been glitched by Kevin Ryan. Original photograph by Andrew Mager (CC BY-SA 2.0).

The pieces contained within this work are fiction. Names, characters, places, and incidents are the product of the author's imagination; any resemblance to actual persons, living or dead, events, or locales is entirely coincidental.

The information in this book is distributed on an "as is" basis, without warranty. Although every precaution has been taken in the preparation of this work, neither the authors nor the publisher shall have any liability to any person or entity with respect to any loss or damage caused or alleged to be caused directly or indirectly by the information contained in this book.

Table of Contents

// WRITING // #CYBERPUNKNEAR

// FOCUS ON EPUBLISHING

// ART

// MORE FROM THE LONDON READER

LR

#cyberpunkNOW is dedicated to the memory of
Lukas Mariman
1972 – 2016

About
The London Reader

E ACH VOLUME of the London Reader features the work and thoughts of contemporary voices in creative writing. Pieces are selected and introduced by a curator, as in a gallery, to explore a single theme, genre, region, or topic. Each volume is cooperatively owned by all collaborators and contributors. The revenue from your subscription directly supports the writers you love to read.

Find the London Reader
- online at **www.LondonReader.uk**
- on Twitter **@LondonReaderMag**
- on Facebook at **@LondonReaderMag**

Become a subscriber
- to the Kindle edition in the UK: **www.amzn.to/2fvO7Th**
- to the Kindle edition in the US: **www.amzn.to/2gDSdG6**
- to the print or pdf edition anywhere in the world: **www.patreon.com/LondonReader**

If you have comments, questions, or suggestions, contact the London Reader at **coordinator@LondonReader.uk**

LR

#cyberpunkNOW

Curated by

Alexander H Maurice

I N 1990 THE UNITED STATES SECRET SERVICE raided the office of Steve Jackson Games in Austin, Texas. Steve Jackson Games produced roleplaying and board games, one of which was the forthcoming GURPS Cyberpunk, inspired by the novels and short stories of William Gibson, Bruce Sterling, and others. The cyberpunk game manuscripts and computers were seized by the Secret Service as part of an investigation into a criminal intrusion—or hack—into Bell South's computer systems. In an ironic twist ending, it was a haunting herald of the millennium to come. The future tech dystopia imagined by cyberpunk authors had fast become reality.

This year marks twenty-five years since the World Wide Web was first made available to the public. Access to the Internet is now argued to be part of the human right to communicate. The average Brit spends close to three hours a day online; yet while the web has revolutionized communication and taken up so much of the world's time, it has come with a dystopian underside.

Since 9/11 we've seen a war-like expansion into cyberspace by the world's intelligence agencies. The funding of America's 16 spy agencies has more than doubled in that time. It is fair to say the repercussions of this were only partly revealed in Edward Snowden's leaks about the NSA's surveillance of the world's data and communications. It is not just governments collecting mass data from their citizens. As the renowned computer security expert Bruce Schneier has pointed out, "Surveillance is the business model of the Internet." Corporations harvest data from their users in order to sell it to advertisers. Search engine and social media companies are the intelligence agencies of the 21st Century. While corporations are harvesting this information for their own profit, we have seen incidents around the world where they have worked hand-in-glove with government agencies, freely sharing users' information. This collusion between big business and big intelligence has led to the arrests of protesters, dissidents, and even media pirates guilty only of downloading a movie.

The dystopian visions of the cyberpunk authors of the 80s are coalescing around us. Technological interconnectedness has enveloped the world while wealth inequality has hit record levels in the West. Over 2 billion people connect to the Internet through their phones, everyone from CEOs to refugees, yet there is substantially more of the latter. Globally one in every 113 people is displaced by conflict, the highest number since the mass devastation of second world war. As record numbers of people have drowned in the Mediterranean trying to escape conflict—almost 3,000 in the first half of 2016—Europe has become increasing entrenched in walls and razor wire.

And yet technology trickles down from Silicon Valley. 2016 also saw the explosion of augmented reality, with hordes of people roaming around parks hunting imaginary creatures on one of the most downloaded smartphone apps. The dystopian future predicted in the fiction of the 80s, of high technology and inequality, is proving more and more prescient.

In her Cyborg Manifesto, published in 1985, professor and theorist Donna Haraway boldly declared, "We are cyborgs—theorized and fabricated hybrids of machine and organism." That is more obvious now than ever, when access to our smartphones has become programmed in the muscle memory of our fingers.

In this volume of the London Reader, which is fittingly our inaugural digital volume, we will reflect on this present dystopian moment through the lens of the heady and prophetic genre fiction of the 1980s: cyberpunk. These are stories of high technology and inequality while their characters are pushed to the peripheries as corporations and government agencies vie for power. We're more interconnected than ever, but how have these technologies impacted our lives and shaped our connections?

Cyberpunk focuses on "high tech, low life"—or, as Lawrence Person, the editor of the award winning sci-fi magazine Nova Express, describes it, "Classic cyberpunk characters were marginalized, alienated loners who lived on the edge of society in generally dystopian futures where daily life was impacted by rapid technological change [and] an ubiquitous datasphere of computerized information."

In this volume we will use the genre to provide 'cognitive estrangement', to borrow a term from Bruce Sterling, by putting on a pair of cyberpunk mirrorshades to look out at our contemporary world through new lenses.

This volume features interviews with two of the founders of cyberpunk, William Gibson and Bruce Sterling, as well as the award winning science fiction author Kim Stanley Robinson. They look back on the genre and reflect on the state of the world now (#cyberpunkGREATS #scifiGREATS). Minifiction from Benn Ward, Zak Kain, Francine Brewer, and Reishi Rousseau, poetry by Dann Was, and a short story by Will Cerbone all explore our contemporary world through cyberpunk lenses (#cyberpunkNOW). Venturing ahead, short stories by Lena Ng and George Bartlett and a piece of minifiction by AM Hayward look cautiously forward from the funk of the present with a worried and yet sometimes optimistic eye for the future (#cyberpunkNEAR). The genre is visually represented in this volume by art from the graffiti artist Core246 and the digital artist Shinji Toya, who has recently exhibited at the Tate Modern in London. Both of these artists reflect our contemporary world through a broken black mirror. And finally, with a focus on e-publishing, we explore the mainstream of the genre from best-selling ebook Science Fiction author, Ike Hamill.

Whether you choose to read the interviews, fiction, and poetry in the order presented or by clicking about, I hope that you enjoy this volume as much as I enjoyed curating it and that it gives you pause to reflect on our increasingly cyberpunk world and our dystopian moment.

// BIO // Alexander H Maurice has been a writer, journalist, the London Correspondent and Book Reviewer for the Global Intelligence, and one of the editors of the London Reader.

// In his role as researcher and analyst at the Global Intelligence, Maurice has written about the geopolitics of our increasingly digital world, including about state cyberpower, the NSA's mass surveillance program, US extradition attempts of UK hackers, artificial intelligence, global trade deals and Wikileaks, the rise of militarised police forces, the rise of fascism, and the role of troll armies in influencing elections and policy (even before the 2016 election).

// He is also published in Spank! Magazine. He is engaged in the London activist scene, is addicted to his smartphone, and has finally got end-to-end encryption.

LR

Charitable Cause
Help Refugees

A S DESIGNATED by the curator, 10 percent of the revenue from this issue is donated to the Help Refugees registered charity, which grew out of the #helpcalais hashtag. Among other initiatives, Help Refugees has delivered over 300 sleeping bags every week to camps in Europe.

Find out more at **helprefugees.org.uk**

//

Each volume of the London Reader has a different charitable cause chosen based on the issue's focus. Other volumes of the London Reader have raised money for Women's Aid; Right to Play; GiveDirectly, Samaritans, UK; the Castle Art Project at the Akré Refugee Camp in Erbil, Iraq; Cool Earth; and the Rainbow Mission Foundation in Hungary. Each volume of the London Reader you purchase helps support worthwhile causes.

LR

William Gibson

#cyberpunkGREATS #interview

Alexander H Maurice

C ASE WAS TWENTY-FOUR. At twenty-two, he'd been a cowboy, a rustler, one of the best in the Sprawl. He'd been trained by the best, by McCoy Pauley and Bobby Quine, legends in the biz. He'd operated on an almost permanent adrenaline high, a by-product of youth and proficiency, jacked into a custom cyberspace deck that projected his disembodied consciousness into the consensual hallucination that was the matrix. A thief, he'd worked for other, wealthier thieves, employers who provided the exotic software required to penetrate the bright walls of corporate systems, opening windows into rich fields of data.

//

"The matrix has its roots in primitive arcade games," said the voice-over, "in early graphics programs and military experimentation with cranial jacks." On the Sony, a two-dimensional space war faded behind a forest of mathematically generated ferns, demonstrating the spacial possibilities of logarithmic spirals; cold blue military footage burned through, lab animals wired into test systems, helmets feeding into fire control circuits of tanks and war planes. "Cyberspace. A consensual hallucination experienced daily by billions of legitimate operators, in every nation, by children being taught mathematical concepts . . . A graphic representation of data abstracted from the banks of every computer in the human system. Unthinkable complexity. Lines of light ranged in the nonspace of the mind, clusters and constellations of data. Like city lights, receding..."

"What's that?" Molly asked, as he flipped the channel selector.

"Kid's show." A discontinuous flood of images as the selector cycled. "Off," he said to the Hosaka.

Excerpts from Neuromancer (1984)

//

William Gibson has been called one of the founders of cyberpunk. His ground-breaking 1984 novel, Neuromancer, launched the genre into the public consciousness and, in doing so, won the sci-fi "triple crown" of the Nebula, Hugo, and Philip K Dick Awards. The Guardian has described Gibson as "probably the most important novelist of the past two decades." In his 1982 short story, "Burning Chrome", he coined the term 'cyberspace' to refer to the "mass consensual hallucination" of computer systems. He further explored the concept of cyberspace in Neuromancer, the novel in which he prefigured the importance the internet would come to have in our lives. He followed up on its success with two more novels in the same series that would come to form the Sprawl trilogy and went on to write two more trilogies. The Peripheral is his most recent novel. We caught up with William Gibson to ask him about the world he imagined and how we've come to live it.

The London Reader: I've spent time in squats in London where I have looked around to see a room filled with squatters with half shaved heads or dyed hair all locked onto their devices. Second hand smart phones. Loud laptops covered in anti-fascist and no-borders stickers. And I think, here I am living in the world William Gibson imagined years ago. A world that would have been inconceivable to someone 50 years ago. How does it feel seeing the world that you imagined become reality?

William Gibson: I don't think that what I imagined became reality, so much as that the bits of 1977 (or whenever) that I recognized, in a particular way, turned out to have the legs necessary to walk into the future. Squatters, shaved heads, dyed hair, people engrossed in the digital

—all of that was present, or almost present, in 1977. It just hadn't been distributed as evenly as it now has.

LR: You've commented before that cyberspace has become more fully integrated into our physical world, and is no longer a separate space. With smartphones, social media, and augmented reality games like Pokemon Go, what are your thoughts on the ever increasing ways in which we are now living in a 'cyberspace'? Where do you see these technologies taking us next?

William Gibson: I don't actually have "thoughts", that way. I just write. My day to day life, aside from writing, has a sort of anthropological cast to it, though. I watch myself using devices, systems. I watch other people. My fiction isn't an attempt to teach anyone about some body of theory I have about where history is going. That's what people thought SF was about when I was a kid. I'm trying to get a *naturalistic* prose take (in the Early Modernist sense of literary Naturalism) on an inherently fantastic techno-sociological *present*, whether or not I'm ostensibly writing about an imaginary future. When I meet non-literary futurologists, scenario-generators for large corporations, I'm interested in what they do, but it's very obvious to me that it's not at all what I do. Which I imagine isn't true of a lot of science fiction writers.

That isn't what I do, except as a sort of side-effect of my fiction, as I write. It isn't as though I have intimations of what will happen next, which I then contrive to surround with elements of fiction. The book I'm writing now could probably be read as being about where Siri-style AI may go, but it isn't. It's about the various sorts of agency our personal technology (including firearms) already affords us. Though that gives the impression that I write books "about something". I suppose I do, but I'm not aware of what it is while writing them, and my sense of what they might be about depends mainly on subsequent feedback from readers.

LR: In your most recent book, The Peripheral, you explore how people in the future might look back on the past. With our mass documentation, the present era is becoming increasingly transparent to future historians. How do you think people in a 22nd century Europe might look back on people walking around their cities hunting virtual creatures while the refugee crisis unfolds and thousands of people are dying in the Mediterranean each year?

William Gibson: I doubt it will amaze them. If I could know one thing about what the future thinks, it would be how they view us is unlikely to be how we view ourselves now. Think of how the Victorians regarded themselves, as opposed to how we now regard them. We actually know much more about history *prior* to the Victorians than they were able to know. History is a speculative discipline, subject to constant revision. Knowing what the future thinks of us would probably tell us more about ourselves than we'd really want to know.

LR: In your novel Spook Country, several characters are in possession of files that, were they to reveal them, would lead to the public questioning the United States' involvement in the Iraq War. You wrote this years before the claims of Saddam's WMDs turned out to be based on faulty intelligence. Would you have written Spook Country differently knowing what we know from the intervening years, including the recent release of the Chilcot Inquiry and Snowden's revelations about the extent of NSA and GCHQ mass spying? It seems, much more so than when you wrote it, that we're now living in a spook country.

William Gibson: The WMD claims had been disproved before I wrote Spook Country, at least to my own satisfaction, and there was a ubiquitous cultural assumption that the CIA (or whoever) had access to absolutely everything. In Spook Country, Bigend assumes that the NSA can listen in on anyone's telephone conversations. In the year the book was written, the year prior to its publication, I assumed that this was taken, colloquially at least, quite for granted. Spook Country is set in the year prior to its publication. As is each of the Bigend books. So I suppose you could say we're still living in Spook Country. Except that the London of those books, pre-Brexit, I imagine, is now receding rapidly in the mirror.

LR: Again in Spook Country you have a great line where a character is nostalgic for the time when "grown-ups still ran things." I guess this was a sharp barb aimed squarely at Bush; however, it seems all the more pertinent now in what has been called the "post-fact era" with Trump the Republican presidential candidate and across the ocean Boris Johnson leading the Brexit campaign and then being appointed Foreign Secretary. Do you long for a time when grown-ups still ran things, and where do you think we're headed with these adult children at the helm?

William Gibson: I imagine that Bigend could have imagined Trump, but I couldn't, at the time. I think that's actually an indication of how *optimistic* I am, really. How non-dystopian. Compared to Trump, Bush II looks like a statesman. But Trump is no anomaly. He is there because the strategy of the Republican Party, following the resounding defeat of Barry Goldwater in my early teens, cumulatively created a negative space which only a Trump could fill. Their "Southern strategy" of becoming the party of systemic racism, their embrace of evangelical Christianity, all led to Trump, or in any case to the Trump-like. I doubt we'll see the end of the Trump-like any time soon. My dread is the advent of an American authoritarian demagogue who is neither absolutely ignorant nor crazier than a sack full of assholes.

LR: In describing writing Neuromancer, you said, "in 1977, facing first-time parenthood and an absolute lack of enthusiasm for anything like 'career,' I found myself dusting off my twelve-year-old's interest in science fiction. Simultaneously, weird noises were being heard from New York and London. I took Punk to be the detonation of some slow-fused projectile buried deep in society's flank a decade earlier, and I took it to be, somehow, a sign." Do you think that part of that slow-fused projectile hasn't exploded yet and is still burning somewhere in the soul of our society, ready to go off? I'm thinking now of movements like Occupy and #BlackLivesMatter, as well as the London riots and Grime music.

William Gibson: I didn't do much, writing-wise, in 1977. I was too busy observing punk. Which I was too old to feel a part of. One of the things I observed was the relative speed with which the subculture was commodified. Much more quickly than the Sixties counterculture I came up in. Not as quickly as the subsequent grunge, though. If bohemias, as Bruce Sterling says, have been the dreamtime of industrial civilization, are we still industrial enough to have them, in the same sense? I'm inclined to doubt we are. There seems to be no time now for anything to be an undiscovered backwater. Subcultures are harvested for commodification as soon as they're discovered. They are, in effect, veal. I think the BLM movement is very interestingly different, though, because it isn't a bohemia, a subculture. And I'm yet to see it commodified.

LR: Class divide comes up in many of your novels. Neuromancer was written over 30 years ago and since then we've seen a widening wealth gap and a public awareness of the 1%. You've said before that you've seen our society becoming more Victorian in this regard. What drew you to explore inequality when you wrote Neuromancer, and to keep revisiting it?

William Gibson: My awareness of class stems from my childhood in the American south. The white south had (and still has, though I hope to some lesser degree) a class system much more like England's. A caste system, actually. Without which white racism in the United States can't be fully understood. When I began to write SF, I had a sort of shopping list of important things that SF, particularly American SF, seldom seemed concerned with, and class was near the top. Again, literary naturalism.

LR: We've seen increases in technology both increase our freedom —such as allowing social movements to organise and get out on the street, or providing access to mapping and communication to refugees in dangerous situations—as well as limit our freedom due to things like increased government surveillance. We've seen elements of this in many of your books. Is there a balance between the freedom-enhancing and authoritarian uses of technology, or are we slipping to one side?

William Gibson: One key idea about technology, for me, is that we've now very little idea of what people will actually *do* with a given technology until they get their hands on it, and that will determine its actual course as a change-driver, often to the complete surprise of its developers. This was also true of railroads and the telegraph, but differently. Smartphones, for instance, made UFOs go away, and produced a shocking uptick in police murdering black people in the United States. Neither were planned by anyone. So, really, in my view, there's just no telling.

LR: The literary critic and political theorist, Fredric Jameson, has cited cyberpunk as the supreme literary expression of late capitalism. This seems more pertinent now than ever in this time of financial, environmental, and humanitarian crises. As the world becomes more and more "cyberpunk", where do you think the genre is heading?

William Gibson: Being told that anything one does is the supreme literary expression of anything at all induces eye-rolling, in me at least! I was never happy with "cyberpunk" as a label, at all, and I think that it enabled mainstream SF to safely encapsulate what it rightly saw as a subversive influence. Embrace the subversive, draw it near, declare it a subgenre. But I think that "cyberpunk", so-called, has by now managed to produce several large and quite interestingly unseemly excrescences of the bole of SF's genre-tree, perhaps to the extent that one day the tree may be thought to have always been gnarled that way.

LR

Bruce Sterling

#cyberpunkGREATS #interview

Alexander H Maurice

J ANE GAZED THOUGHTFULLY at the twenty-thousand-meter thunderhead rising on the horizon ahead of her and wondered if there'd ever been a time when it was a whole lot of good clean fun to have money. Maybe back before the heavy weather hit, back when the world was quiet and orderly. Back before the 'information economy' blew up and fell down in the faces of its eager zealot creators, just like communism. Back when there were stable and workable national currencies. And stock markets that didn't fluctuate insanely. And banks that belonged to countries and obeyed laws, instead of global pirate banks that existed nowhere in particular and made up their own laws out of chickenwire dishes, encryption, and spit.

//

He kicked the paper suit off his feet, then stood on top of the paper and pulled off his right shoe. 'The border is fucked, and the government is fucked!' He pulled off the left shoe and flung it aside. 'And society is fucked, and the climate is *really* fucked. And the media are fucked, and the economy is fucked, and the smartest people in the world live like refugees and criminals!' He ripped the plasticwrap off a pair of patterned silk boxer shorts and stepped into them. 'And nobody has *any* idea how to make things any better, and there *isn't* any way to make things better, and there isn't gonna *be* any way, and we don't control *anything* important about our lives! And that's just how it is today, and yes, it's funny!' He laughed shrilly. 'It's hilarious!

And if you don't get the joke, you don't deserve to be alive in the 2030s.'

Excerpts from Heavy Weather (1994)

//

Bruce Sterling is another of cyberpunk's founding fathers. His Mirrorshades anthology helped position cyberpunk as a movement in science fiction. He has written 12 novels and many short stories, the most notable of which is Islands in the Net, which won the Campbell Award in 1989. He has been a professor at the European Graduate School and a "visionary in residence" at the Art Centre College of Design in Pasadena, California. He has also coined many neologisms, including 'buckyjunk', 'slipstream', 'spime', and 'major consensus narrative'. He is also the author of the recent novel, Pirate Utopia, described by Michael Moorcock as "a wild satire about serious issues". We caught up with Sterling to ask him about his novels and to weigh in on our dystopian moment.

The London Reader: We're living in a world that would have been inconceivable to many 30 years ago. How does it feel seeing the world that you imagined become reality?

Bruce Sterling: That depends on what aspect of the world has changed in front of my eyes. You'd think that the experience might feel pretty weird, but a lot of it is rather slow, gentle, and melancholy. Watching myself and friends get old (and I always knew that would happen) it's profound and inexorable. Watching cities get bigger, well, cities certainly do, but urbanization has been happening during my entire lifetime, so it's not a shock. Watching the climate crisis savaging the planet's surface is truly horrifying. I never wanted that to get real, and boy, is it ever.

Some things that I imagine do become "reality" for just a few seasons, and then become the past. I can well imagine some object or service, and it might get more or less realized, but it still becomes obsolete. I used to write a lot of glowing verbiage about fax machines.

I'm pretty good at spotting trends, especially technical ones, but I don't put a lot of stock in my broad-scale abilities as a cultural visionary. So it truly interests me to see stuff that JG Ballard imagined becoming reality (for a little while, anyway).

LR: Your novel The Zenith Angle, which came out in 2004 and takes place after 9/11, describes a computer security expert working for a wing of the United States government. Would you have written it any differently following the Snowden Revelations?

Bruce Sterling: Probably not, no. The book's a technothriller that's based on programming rather than espionage. Also, I read James Bamford's books on the NSA, so the Snowden revelations weren't all that startling and amazing to me. Mostly it was the level of gritty detail in the Snowden documents that was so intense, embarrassing, and polarizing. Also Snowden himself is quite an interesting historical figure. He successfully carried out a daring, larger-than-life political act as a moral dissident. He hasn't revealed anything shocking lately, but his stature continues to grow.

It's hard to publish a genre technothriller that isn't basically about the right-wing awe and wonder of financing advanced Pentagon weapons systems. In the long-term those creations are rarely all that thrilling.

LR: In your 1988 novel Islands in the Net you describe an assassination by drone and a world police called the Free Army of Counter-Terrorism, which feels a bit uncanny now. How do you feel looking back on your work from the context of our contemporary war on terror and unilateral drone assassinations?

Bruce Sterling: It didn't take Nostradamus to figure out that drones would covertly kill people. There were plenty of operations-other-than-war going on in the 1980s and drones were already buzzing around. They were just smaller and more primitive drones than ours.

Today, the most unusual aspect of Islands in the Net is that the book describes an effective world police. The book features an armed globalising force supporting a new international world political order, called the "Vienna Convention". We've got pretty much no stabilizing "global order" force like that nowadays. A few Norwegian guys in UN blue helmets blowing whistles, that's about it. Terrorists, oligarch hot-money, and crazy political movements detached from objective reality, we've sure got plenty of those, though.

It's pretty easy to get a reputation for accurately "predicting the future" when you can dramatize little-known real-world activities that are already present. HG Wells used to say that it worked best if you chose just one obscure novelty for one story and then tripled the size of it. Personally, I think science fiction works even better when it picks huge topics that people are unable to honestly confront. The future has a freight of the unimaginable, but it's chock-full of the unmentionable.

LR: Your novel, Heavy Weather, published in 1994, describes storm chasers who pilot drones into mega storms caused by athropogenic climate change. After Hurricane Katrina and now, in what is set to be the hottest year on record, this feels particularly prophetic. You revisited the dangers of climate change in your closing remarks at SXSW recently. Considering the weak targets agreed upon at COP21, do you think we will be able to address climate change, or are we doomed to the future you depict in Heavy Weather?

Bruce Sterling: We're already in climate crisis. The 'doom,' such as it is, is upon us. The present resembles Heavy Weather less than it resembles other science fiction books written in the 1990s that failed to mention the climate crisis, but that's not a great feat. Climate-crisis reality today doesn't look much like the fictional climate-crisis future imagined twenty years ago in Heavy Weather.

We're gonna spend the rest of our lives in a worsening climate crisis. It's mostly about stacking the sandbags and trying to somehow make the crisis less-worse than it's already bound to get. Unlike other "ages", like the Atomic Age and the Space Age, there's gonna be no easy way out of the carbon-dioxide pollution age.

Even *if* COP21 had passed all kinds of sharp targets, COP21 still has to rely on national governments to carry out its ideal suggestions. We don't have any national governments with that effective talent and ability. None. National leaders can't resolve minor global issues like a banking crisis, much less rewiring the entire planet in real-time. We're in a condition of failed globalization, and nation-states like Britain, and confederacies like Europe, are similarly failing, for the same reasons.

LR: I gather from your comments in your closing remarks at SXSW that you're not a fan of bitcoin, but do you see the potential for something such as a universal basic income created by a blockchain currency?

Bruce Sterling: Sure, the blockchain's got technical potential, but its political and social design as a form of wealth is a coder's fantasy. That's why Bitcoiners get ripped off and taken to the cleaners every day. Trying to use crypto-code to protect your wealth is like trying to build a picket fence around your house with one picket a mile high. Money isn't merely ones and zeroes; money's "attack surface" is huge. When there's no law and order to repress the malefactors, even Secret Service agents are gonna break down and steal.

All you have to do is look at the personal morality of people involved in Bitcoin in order to know the enterprise won't end well. Obviously they're covert, sleazy, back-biting, piratical characters with zero interest in genuine prosperity. Once a month or so, I witness something horrible happening to one of these blockchain hucksters. They're gonna continue to internally wrangle over their precious code, and they're gonna continue to go to jail, get humiliated, lose millions instantly to blackhats and have to crawl to the FBI, get outmanoeuvred by Chinese money-launderers, peddle drugs and get stuck in prison for life by angry New York Feds who police the fiat banking system. Man, it's been a loathsome spectacle.

On the guaranteed annual income front, that scheme may have some legs. In a world of negative interest rates, even just giving consumers bundles of cash out of helicopters makes more sense than what's been done since 2008. Basically, though, a guaranteed annual income is just "welfare" for everybody. Being on welfare had unpleasant, degrading aspects even when it was gaudy bread-and-circuses in the ancient Roman Empire.

I would take a free pension cheerfully, but I rather imagine it would just substitute a new set of social problems for the acute ones we already have. The ancient Greeks would probably tell us that our money-mad society fails because we lack any interest in justice.

LR: You've said that you don't think that our concerns about government and corporate surveillance is as big deal as we think it is and that despite so much government surveillance, the intelligence agencies don't seem to know anything. However, the increasing digitization of our communications has weaknesses. In some of my research, I have argued that in the big data competition between the NSA and Google, it is only a matter of time before either the U.S. Government or private entities have the power to manipulate populations at home or abroad not unlike how China does behind its great firewall. What keeps you optimistic about the future of privacy and surveillance?

Bruce Sterling: I never claimed I was "optimistic". I just said that probably surveillance wasn't as big a deal as guys like you think it is. Because, if you surveil somebody, you still need the capacity to act in order to repress them. And if you had that capacity to act decisively—why wouldn't you arrest everybody at Google and the NSA immediately? Obviously they're a bigger political threat to anybody else, so why not just liquidate them all? Most genuine surveillance societies are racked with purges inside the political spy elite. Surveillance societies aren't strong, they're weak because they're secretive and paranoid.

China's Great Firewall is truly an impressive achievement and probably the avant-garde for the next phase of post-global "cyberspace sovereignty" of the balkanized post-Internet. But betting on Chinese political stability makes no historical sense. The Chinese are keen on palace intrigues that become civil wars and have always been their own worst enemies. The Chinese have certainly got better hardware nowadays, but the whole point of their Great Firewall is to loudly insist that they're still plenty Chinese.

LR: In your short story "Junk DNA" one of your characters, commenting on another character's 'killer app' tells them that they're going to be "bigger than Pokemon". That takes on whole new significance now. You've spoken extensively on Augmented Reality (AR) before, but it's only recently we've seen mobs of people in parks, glued to their phones, hunting Pokemon. What are your thoughts on the ever increasing ways in which AR will impact our lives?

Bruce Sterling: I like Pokemon. I never play it, but its design as a transmedia game that is also a kid's economics is really intriguing and impressive. Also, I'm a Nipponophile and its globalised Japanese-ness appeals to me.

I also really like augmented reality, I have a long-lasting fondness for it, but to date there's never been an augmentation application with big "impact". Augments are more like visual street art, paste-on stickers, little hopping cartoons. In some ways, I rather hope they stay in that amusement quadrant, because it might get pretty hairy to see a world where serious everyday players like cops, soldiers, doctors, teachers, and engineers are maintaining our world by using phantoms in front of their eyes.

Imagine a world where Mom goes to the crib first thing in the morning, puts on her glasses and scans the baby. That would be genuine AR "impact", but that's quite a different world than ours.

LR: As the world has become more and more "cyberpunk", what do you think is left for the genre?

Bruce Sterling: I'm frankly more worried about what's left for late capitalism. [Frederic] Jameson was probably right to say that cyberpunk was tied into a particular kind of 80s-90s Washington Consensus economic model. But that model doesn't work at all nowadays, and it's pretty hard to get "supreme literary expressions" when there's no cash around for writers and nobody's got spare screenless hours for tl;dr leisure reading.

The genre's quite a peculiar institution now. Personally, I like writing Italian *fantascienza*. Compared to American science fiction, where there's still some money and a lot of vicious political trolling around, Italian *fantascienza* seems quite low-key and civilized. I wouldn't say that everyone working in American science fiction ought to drift off toward Italy, but it's something that characters in most Bruce Sterling SF novels would have done cheerfully.

I've always been a sci-fi ideologue and I have plenty of avuncular advice for people in the genre, but I'd be more impressed if somebody in the genre just amazed and surprised me. That could happen. It's happened before.

LR: And finally, you have a new novel, Pirate Utopia, that will be out by the time this is published. What can you tell us about it?

Bruce Sterling: Pirate Utopia is a work of *fantascienza*. It's not a big novel, just a novella, but I think it's pretty good; it's interesting because it's a detailed literary engagement with a truly weird and scary episode of European political extremism. It's also quite the sort of thing Bruce Sterling would have written as a native Italian writer. I find it personally satisfying to be able to respond to that kind of expressive opportunity.

Pirate Utopia is set in the year 1920. I like going back and forth in time for topics, but I also like going across the grain in cultures. As a science fiction writer, I'm always on some quest for "cognitive estrangement", for "making it new". I think a good working fantasist will do a better job of fantasy when they don't sit all alone in their studios making up long lists of trolls and elves. Reality is so much more fantastic than any single person can imagine. As an effective artist, you've got to somehow find the courage to abandon that comfy desk and venture out and steal stuff from people.

LR

Kim Stanley Robinson

#scifiGREATS #interview

Alexander H Maurice

KIM STANLEY ROBINSON is the best-selling science fiction author of nineteen novels, including the Mars, Science in the Capital, and Three Californias trilogies. According to the New Yorker, he is "generally acknowledged as one of the greatest living science-fiction writers". He has won many awards, including the Nebula Award for Best Novel, the Hugo Award for Best Novel, and the World Fantasy Award. His novels frequently explore ecological sustainability and inequality and often feature scientists as heroes. His 1988 cyberpunk novel The Gold Coast, explores a dystopian future featuring "an endless sprawl of condos, freeways, and malls" and anti-arms industry terrorism, sex, and drugs. We caught up with Kim Stanley Robinson to ask him about his novels, about the state of the world, and about where to look forward from here.

The London Reader: You have said that you have a natural tendency towards realism but that if you're going to write about our world, science fiction is the best genre with which to do that. What are some insights you think science fiction can give us about the state of our contemporary world?

Kim Stanley Robinson: SF suggests that change will happen because history doesn't stop; also that the moment we're in has been created by people in response to their situation, and that process keeps going on. This is the most powerful general insight that reading SF gives. Then also it's good at dramatizing the incredible spread of futures that are possible from the current moment, ranging from a very bad mass extinction event (dystopia) to a very impressive and exciting civilization on a healthy planet (utopia). That's a good reminder of how important our choices now are, in shaping the opportunities our descendants will have. Making all that vivid is so useful, even important, that all SF can be regarded as a kind of utopian effort, or at least a strong tool for thinking historically.

LR: You've said, "Either you're an environmentalist, or you're not paying attention." The environment is a key issue that you keep returning to in your fiction. In what is set to be the hottest year on record, are you optimistic or pessimistic about humanity's ability to effectively address climate change?

Kim Stanley Robinson: I'm not sure I actually said that, but whatever; what I would say is that the term "environmentalist" is odd and restrictive and comes from an earlier paradigm, in which "the environment" was seen as something outside of us and in some sense a luxury, which certain prosperous people could afford to advocate as a kind extra beyond the necessities. The framing is wrong here, and that word "environmentalist" is to an extent an attempt to box "environmentalism" into a set of political choices that are like a menu of options that one can choose to advocate or not.

It's better to rethink all this and regard the planet's biosphere as an extension of our bodies, or the most extensive parts of our bodies, so that simple self-regard for our own health includes taking care of these extensive parts of us. So, either you acknowledge this newly-emerging physical and biological reality, or you're not paying attention to all the latest information coming in from all the sciences. That would be a better way to put it. We are part of our biosphere and depend crucially on it for our own health.

So then, my optimism is a matter of policy. I choose optimism as a matter of obligation to the generations to come. The Earth is heating up now by a rate of .6 watts per square meter right now, it's a big load. We have the power to reduce that growing heat load pretty rapidly, and efforts are being made to do that, and more needs to be done. It will be the overriding story of this century in terms of civilization's relationship to the planet. Ecological damage will be done, there will be extinctions; progress will be made, we will decarbonize. It's a mess but we are actually working on it now, so that's a positive sign. But more has to be done.

LR: You've also said that science and capitalism are in conflict. Could you elaborate on that?

Kim Stanley Robinson: They are conjoined twins in conflict for control of history. Science is about studying the world in the hope of reducing suffering, increasing our power in the physical world, and keeping the planet healthy. Capitalism is about the few exploiting the many in the pursuit of unnecessary toxic wealth.

Over-simple? Manichean? A kind of puppet play, as in some sort of mythology? Yes. But it's right, too. So we have to deal. Because people with capital can buy governments, and even buy the results of science and the directions it works in. So the fight is on, and people have to choose sides.

LR: In your Mars trilogy you describe capitalism as an outgrowth of feudalism and you explore some alternatives to capitalism. Do you view these as possible ways forward from the crises of late capitalism? Or how do you see us escaping from one of the central crises of capitalism, what you describe as the need for perpetual growth versus our limited biosphere?

Kim Stanley Robinson: Ideas about possible post-capitalist political economies are fairly limited, I've found. They steer between the poles of being innovative but unrealistic in terms of actually implementing them or being plausible but insufficient to deal with the problems we face.

The way I see it happening is by a series of reforms of capitalism leading in gradual contested steps to some kind of post-capitalist system. Because we can't grow the economy endlessly, we won't. Growth will be redefined as improvement, maybe by involution or simplification or design improvement or cultural shifts in what we desire, or all these. The two great problems of capitalism, wrecking people's lives and wrecking the biosphere, can both be improved by treating the necessities and the biosphere as things more valuable than money, beyond price, and there-fore to be attended to by civilization action (government) rather than profit motives. We have to arrange to give ourselves decent livings in re-turn for keeping the biosphere healthy. The current economic system doesn't do that because it values and prices things wrong, but we could do it. It's physically possible.

LR: In your 2005 novel, Fifty Degrees Below, you explore the threat of total surveillance. Since then, thanks to the Snowden revela-tions, we've seen the extent to which we are living in a state of total sur-veillance. In a way, reality has overtaken your fiction. Were you sur-prised? And would you have written Fifty Degrees Below any differently after the NSA leaks?

Kim Stanley Robinson: I was not surprised at the idea of the NSA doing surveillance, but it was surprising how long it went on without be-ing revealed. Ultimately Snowden did us an important service and he and other whistle-blowers and leakers should be regarded as heroic fig-ures, no matter their personal flaws or mistakes; nobody's perfect. The supposed danger their revelations put some people in was mostly myth-ical, and if real were often dangers created by bad action in the first place. As for Fifty Degrees Below, I would not rewrite it now—it still seems a good description of our moment, or good enough to be provoc-ative.

LR: Even though fiction is broadly seen as escapism, cyberpunk and science fiction often address important political issues. What role do you see fiction authors playing in the political discourse?

Kim Stanley Robinson: First I want to say that cyberpunk is a sub-genre of science fiction, not a separate thing as your question implies. It is the primary science fiction mode of the 1980s, and coming after the radical and feminist SF of the 1970s, it was a reactionary and even defeatist form of SF, saying that corporations were going to control everything and we might as well get used to it. This is why cyberpunk was so quickly celebrated by the Wall Street Journal.

As to the role fiction plays in political discourse, it's an important part of the stories we tell ourselves about what matters and who we are. These are always political judgements, so fiction is important. Science fiction gives visions of possible futures, so it too is also always political, and important. [Edward] Bellamy's Looking Backward [published in 1888] was a big part of the progressive moment in American history, and HG Wells' utopian novels help to shape the thinking of the people who created the international order after the second world war. So fiction has this indirect and amorphous but important part to play.

LR: Since cyberpunk first appeared we have seen the growth of corporate power, especially now with recent trade deals such as TPP and TiSA. While the Wall Street Journal may have once celebrated cyberpunk, we've seen grassroots responses to corporations, such as Occupy Wall Street, that seem to grow on a cyberpunk ethos. Certainly a critique of corporations is more pertinent now than ever?

Kim Stanley Robinson: Occupy Wall Street does not exhibit a cyberpunk ethos, which to me seems taken whole cloth from film noir. That was all about getting by in a world that couldn't be changed, where big distant powers ruled. There was no political resistance in either. That Wall Street has subsequently grown even stronger is true, but the lack of a critical and revolutionary literature of resistance in the leading science fiction of the 1980s certainly did nothing to help the situation. You could say cyberpunk succeeded as diagnostic but failed in terms of cognitive mapping or a call to change the system.

LR: While you've dealt with the dystopian consequences of climate change in several of your novels, you also tend to write utopias, such as 2132. Do you feel that is becoming harder given the present state of the world?

Kim Stanley Robinson: Utopias are always equally hard or easy to write. Wells wrote most of his between WWI and WWII, so it couldn't be worse in terms of contemporary circumstances. Utopias are mostly a matter of saying, 'Things could be better, and here's one scenario of how they could be better.' My novel 2312 is as much about 2012 as it is about three hundred years from now, and all SF functions as both a portrait of a possible future and a metaphorical portrait of the present of the time of writing. That double focus creates the 3D effect, of history seen as such, that is one of the strengths of SF.

LR: In your novelette, The Lucky Strike, you explore the moral responsibility and choices facing the Captain tasked with dropping the atomic bomb on Hiroshima and who ultimately decides not to. Does this story reflect your views? That we all must act morally even if ordered to do otherwise?

Kim Stanley Robinson: Yes, I would agree with the statement we all must act morally even if ordered to do otherwise. Or even if doing otherwise is not ordered, but simply presented as normal and fun and the only way to do things. Judgements need to be made about all that, to be a thinking and creative member of society.

LR: Finally, you have a new novel that will be out by the time this is read: New York 2140. What can you tell us about it?

Kim Stanley Robinson: It's a novel describing the world after a sea level rise of about 50 feet, focusing mostly on lower Manhattan and global finance. So naturally it's a utopian comedy.

LR

Twenty-One Brief Moments from an Otherwise Unremarkable Life
#cyberpunkNOW #shortstory
Will Cerbone

// INTRO // After the shooting of police at a recent protest in Austin, Texas, a man who had been openly carrying his registered rifle as a political statement identified himself to police and turned over his gun in order to aid their efforts during the unfolding crisis. The more sensationalist of news outlets hastily announced that he was a suspect in the shooting. Social media turned against him, but even after the misinformation was corrected, the alleyways of the Internet that conspiracy addicts frequent flew into manic analysis trying to connect this seemingly unconnected man to the unfathomable event. A similar series of events unfolded around the Sandy Hook shooter's brother and around a man misidentified as the Boston Marathon Bomber on the cover of the New York Post.

// In the short story "Twenty-One Brief Moments from an Otherwise Unremarkable Life", Will Cerbone was inspired by these incidents to explore the dystopian interaction between the mass hysteria created by terrorism and our increasingly interconnected digital society. He does so through a series of glimpses into the life of one man presented with subtle wit and an ironic detachment that puts the reader equidistant between the absurd and the everyday experiences of Nathan's ordeal.

*// BIO // Will Cerbone is an editor of scholarly books and is based in New York. On twitter he critiques most things at @**lessthanwomprat***

Twenty-One Brief Moments from an Otherwise Unremarkable Life
Will Cerbone

AFTER THE WORST of the violence, as the curfew came into effect and the state of emergency was extended, the police released to the media an unnamed suspect's photograph. The crowdsourced photo shows Nathan smiling, holding a large backpack at his side, in front of a building that (one does have to admit) stood near the epicenter of the attack.

The photograph is more than two years old and depicts Nathan in a state of dishabille, toward the end of a No Shave November during which he had taken on an ungainly appearance in order to raise money for an organisation that offers respite care to the parents of autistic children. The photograph is taken from his profile on a predominant social networking site, publicly available despite the profile's otherwise restrictive privacy settings. When asked, the police decline to identify their source, and so several questions go unanswered. Several commentators on the forums of obscure websites take note.

Concerned citizens—vigilantes or activists—are the first to identify Nathan, and his name is released to the public (if not through official channels). Recriminations pour in on Nathan's social media account, and he answers the first few with confusion and then obscenity. Investigators arrive to interview Nathan in his home, and there the matter is settled to their satisfaction. An apology is offered, and the official media release bearing the photograph is deleted and retracted before Nathan goes to bed.

In the morning, the presumed perpetrators are located and arraigned. On the advice of counsel, they decline to explain their motivations or their goals in any way that is intelligible to the public or the media. News correspondents and media experts dissect some initial, cryptic statements at great length, but they fail to produce satisfying hypotheses. Basic demographic information reveals that the three attackers belong to an ethnic minority whose members are often but not necessarily adherents to a prominent minority religion. The citizens of Nathan's nation are, by and large, unconcerned with this strong correlation, and so the commentators in the media do not find it necessary to discuss any apocalyptic clash of civilizations. The perpetrators are deemed mentally ill (though they will face criminal prosecution, perhaps capital punishment).

Curiously, Nathan (whose address and phone number were leaked, evidently, to a number of clearinghouses for such information) continues to receive admonition and the occasional threat.

A new phase of life has begun.

//

Nathan refuses the first pizza, imagining its delivery to his home to be the result of a poor telephone connection or errant keystroke. The driver is disappointed, but (in a pleasant surprise, given recent events) he accepts Nathan's explanation at face value. Soon, however, a pattern emerges as another driver arrives, and then another. In total, eleven pizzas are sent that first day before every pizza parlour in the neighbourhood has seen its services refused at least once.

Nathan, in a moment of grim humour, accepts the fifth pizza. He hopes to make the best of a bad situation, but he discovers that the pizza has been rendered inedible. Toppings include hot and alfredo sauces, pineapple, anchovies, and ranch and blue cheese salad dressings. For this, Nathan pays more than twice his hourly wage.

//

Perhaps four phone calls arrive per hour from concerned citizens designating Nathan a sonofabitch and things worse. Far more reach out via email and SMS, describing his culpability for unnamed crimes, his sexual orientation, the size of his genitalia, one of several manners of execution appropriate for him, and the addresses of his parents and girlfriend.

//

On the microblogging platform, viewership statistics are tabulated by an algorithm which takes into account the number of users exposed to each post, the rate at which those users engaged with the post, and the length of time that the post continued to be listed and actively served to users. By these metrics, the Impact of the post naming Nathan as a person of interest is an order of magnitude greater than that of its retraction.

These data are provided to the police department's social media co-ordinator in an automated weekly email which no one has ever opened.

//

Some strange corner of the internet remains hungrily suspicious of the irregularities surrounding Nathan being named and cleared by police within a single day. Over weeks and months, accusations against him take more precise form. For their precision, they remain unfalsifiable: Nathan has participated in one of a cornucopia of conspiracies, each undetectable and subtle in purpose, often global in scope. His role has been one of several that can be confirmed by evidence, but neither identified nor refuted. He is neither a bomber nor a gunman nor a radical himself, but a government scapegoat, a crisis actor, a distractor employed by those who wish to usher in a new world order. His denial is confirmation. Denial from any official source would constitute collusion.

Not truly accused, he can offer no true defence of himself, and he opts to withdraw from the avenues to which these strangers enjoy easy access. Only in the course of this inventory of his internet presences does he discover the abuse that has been heaped on his unused handle on a microblogging platform, which has received additional opprobrium and more open threats. He reports those threats promising sexual violence and closes the account.

//

A delivery driver dispatched by a Chinese restaurant at the request of Nathan's girlfriend, Maeve, arrives at his door. Though pizzas have been the primary medium of culinary vigilantism, and though this particular form of intrusion has abated, the gentleman offering the *lo mein* brought to mind the bags of unordered Mexican, Indian, Japanese, Thai, and Middle Eastern cuisine that nonetheless arrived. Nathan's adrenaline explodes just long enough to scream at the driver for his complicity in the ongoing destruction of his life. Maeve and Nathan resolve to cook for themselves more.

//

Within an impressive six months, a streaming-television network police drama depicts the events that thrust Nathan into the public eye, including his false identification by police. Though Nathan's character is initially an object of sympathy, it comes to the attention of investigators that the his character raped a woman by force several years before the events of the episode. By the heroic will of the female lead and the bravery of the guest star, the case is brought to trial, but Nathan's character is acquitted on an infuriating technicality. The female lead attempts to comfort the guest-star victim, but her remarks fail to soothe her, and the episode closes on the female lead's partner remarking that sometimes, they just get away.

Nathan was neither consulted during production nor compensated after the debut. Names had been changed to protect the innocent.

//

At the mall, outside a discount clothing retailer nonetheless popular with upwardly mobile young adults, a stranger identifies Nathan by sight and asks him whether he is a member of the same ethnic minority as the attackers who have indirectly made him a pariah. Nathan responds in the negative, which the stranger characterizes as bullshit before launching into a tirade. Nathan's irrelevance to the attack has abetted a cover-up, and the stranger would like to know how much money Nathan received from national authorities or perhaps the Russian government or the UN. The stranger's female companion becomes embarrassed and drags him away. They fight loudly outside an electronic accessories boutique.

//

On a sleepy Saturday afternoon, having spent the morning attempting to bake cinnamon rolls and then making love and catching up on their favourite television programs via streaming video service, Nathan steels himself to consent to Maeve's request to order takeout. Their chosen online restaurant listing service has added his address to a blacklist due to a series of fraudulent or refused orders—as has its competitors.

//

Due to mishandling of customer data by a national home improvement chain, fifty-six million current and former customers are placed at risk of the loss of their Personally Identifiable Information. Loss, in this context, refers not to the annihilation of this information but to its acquisition by an unauthorized party.

The data lost in the breach are not believed to include unique identifiers such as Social Security Numbers or Credit or Personal Identification Numbers, but nevertheless Nathan discovers that several accounts have been opened in his name.

It is possible that identifying details from the lost dataset were correlated with fragmentary details from a previous breach of another vendor, perhaps a health insurance provider. It is also possible that the information in the home improvement big box leak was used by a determined attacker to access Nathan's customer data at another corporation using social engineering. The customer service representative cannot say with certainty. It is likely that no one, except for the attacker, can. This generally does not happen, unless one is a person of particular interest or celebrity, and then one ought to sign up for a service that denies or complicates credit checks by placing holds that require additional authorizations.

//

During the lengthy dispute process, financing a car proves impossible, renting one merely expensive, and connecting the power at a new apartment a surprising hassle. With some difficulty, now and again Nathan is able to prove to someone's satisfaction that he is himself, but that effort is rewarded with the discovery that such a vouchsafe is not a great comfort to his putative creditors, not while his fraudulent debts remain outstanding.

//

Nathan begs but cannot bring himself to argue against Maeve's decision to leave him. At this, the consummation of a long-building dread, he cannot express genuine surprise, but the relief with which his grief is tinged is too slight to bear the focus of his attention.

Some eleven- to fifteen-hundred first- and second-degree friends, relations, and acquaintances from Nathan and Maeve's college days and earlier become eligible to receive notification of the end of the relationship on social media, subject to the outputs of some algorithms. One such individual, her memory jarred by the vision of Nathan's profile photo, rushes to a web forum dedicated to information-sharing among a community of truth-seekers. There, she sketches a biography of Nathan, detailed to the best of her recollection and bolstered by Moments mined from his social media page. That he has broadcast little news since he came to the attention of that very community is viewed as ironclad confirmation of his general culpability. Delight is taken in the shambles his life has become.

//

A letter from an unknown address arrives, and Nathan sighs with resignation, imagining that his tormentors have at last crossed whatever line had guaranteed that they would deal with him only through unknowing proxies like delivery drivers and the Internet. He nearly does not open it.

In a sensitive, feminine hand, the letter expresses sympathy for his ordeal. A brief biography of the writer follows, along with her contact information and a photograph. She is local.

//

Police arrive at Nathan's home, half-furnished. They protect themselves with riot gear and military-grade armaments. As the door crashes down, Nathan, in abject compliance, falls to the ground face-first and places his hands behind his back. He is handcuffed and stepped over as his remaining possessions are thrown asunder and searched, an ordeal perhaps ninety minutes in length.

Investigators fail to locate the kidnapped child for whom they have searched. Also unlocated is the arsenal purported to be in Nathan's possession. At the station, a sergeant explains that the evening's events have followed from a fraudulent, anonymous report. It is called *swatting*. The sergeant has heard of it, now that he stops to think on it. Kids on the Internet, these days, take things too far. In any case, Nathan is free to go.

//

Nathan and the woman who wrote to him meet and share four intimate encounters before a letter from a second source arrives. He makes inquiries and discovers a fan site devoted to misidentified perpetrators of mass violence, on which his story and mailing address have been posted. The users have rated his physical appearance 4.5/5. The first woman has described Nathan's lovemaking as proficient in narratives both lurid and almost flattering.

He carries on sporadic affairs with three women from the fan site before a persistent itch and a careful examination bring his attention to genital and thigh lesions. To Nathan's partial relief, a nurse-practitioner at the clinic identifies the culprit as pubic lice. The affliction is easily addressed. The nurse remarks that she has been working at the clinic for two years, and this is the first case she has seen. It is hypothesized that trends in pubic grooming have depleted the louse's habitat, like some kind of endangered tern's. Someday, possibly someday very soon, this will be a funny story that Nathan tells.

//

Nathan decides to do just that, to tell his whole story. Publishers respond with form letter rejections, until he reads on the Internet about the proper processes for publication, after which he begins receiving form letter rejections from agents.

One literary and social-media agent is moved by his plight and offers advice. Nathan ought to build up a web presence and then self-publish, using his connections as a marketing base.

//

Having shared several image macros and links to a number of sympathetic news sources on the advice of a woman who is not his literary agent, Nathan treats himself to a short break from work by watching a different woman disrobe at her desk and engage in autoerotic activities as directed by onlookers, and then by masturbating.

Attempting to pay a gratuity to the camgirl, Nathan's web browser presents him with an error indicating that his credit card has been declined. He receives an automated message over SMS warning him that a fraudulent use of his card has been detected. Once contact with his bank has been established by phone and he has confirmed his mother's maiden name, the make and model of the first car he owned, and his first and second job titles and pay scales, Nathan is permitted to confirm that he did intend to transfer what is perhaps a day's post-tax wages through a notorious clearinghouse for pornographers, drug wholesalers, and arms dealers, into the account of Nikki_Redd97.

//

In performing literary research on his colleagues or his competition, Nathan chances on a weblog calling for justice for the victims of the very attack that so affected the course of Nathan's life. The blog writer would achieve this justice through a pogrom against the minority religion to which the members of the ethnic group of the perpetrators often (but do not necessarily) belong. From here, Nathan discovers a ring of interconnected weblogs, forums, and news outlets.

The warmth and compassion of the fellowship Nathan enters into is like nothing he has felt since the attack. He becomes a minor celebrity and builds up a respectable following by writing guest posts on the subject of having one's life destroyed by the religious minority. Life has taken, at last, a positive turn.

//

Nathan is interviewed by the personal stories editor of an internet comedy website whose audience is often (but not necessarily) white, college-educated males, ages 18–35. He and the editor speak over the phone four times, each call lasting over an hour.

The write-up of Nathan's experiences is largely noncritical, with four entries drawn directly from the interviews, indeed presented as long quotations interrupted by periodic stock photography. However, the fifth and final insane thing one learns from being falsely accused of committing a terrorist act is highly editorialized, and the write-up contends that it makes you bugfuck crazy. The editor refers to Nathan's newfound celebrity among white nationalists in negative terms, as though these associations are themselves the outcome of the false accusation and not a remedy to the trauma of that experience.

Nathan receives a modest honorarium for his contribution.

//

On his way to speak at a nationalist rally, checking for traffic on his left side as he merges onto the freeway, it comes to Nathan's attention that his vehicle will require inspection before the first of the next month. Recollections of his previous interactions with the authorities compete aggressively for his attention, and in his distraction he fails to maintain a parity of speed with the flow of traffic. A man in a lime green coup comes up on Nathan's rear bumper, nearly colliding, and he sounds his car horn in what Nathan imagines to be irritation.

Reflexively, Nathan speeds up, but upon reaching the speed limit, he is seized by the fear of attracting attention from an officer tasked with revenue-motivated traffic enforcement, and he slams on his brakes. He does not want to explain his destination. He is breathing heavily now. A nervous energy begins to circulate in his arms, pins and needles, as though they are falling asleep. He does not believe this to be a heart attack and vocally reassures himself of this belief, but this soothes neither his laboured breathing nor the sensations shooting through his extremities.

Pulling off the highway, he turns into the parking lot of a fast food restaurant franchise. He remains in his car and opens the driver's side door. He does not disengage his safety belt until he becomes mindful of how it is adding to his feelings of constriction. Hyperventilating, he exits the car and leans on its hood, which is hot to the touch. He circles the car on foot three times, slowly, keeping a hand on the automobile's frame to steady himself. His head clearer, he gets back inside and drives home.

//

Though Nathan will not recognize it as such, the last encounter directly attributable to these events will occur. His existence and his nefarious activities will have become a footnote among the truth-seekers of the Internet, his name a shibboleth identifying the members of the old guard and the truly obsessive. He will have been deemed defeated, his power to deceive the public destroyed by his exposure. New targets will have emerged.

Seven years after his panic attack on the way to the rally, Nathan will be stepping off a bus in the inner city. A woman who will have been glaring at him for several stops will pass through the exit ahead of him. She will hurl a plastic shopping bag full of takeout refuse at his legs, and the missile will connect and trip him up. Nathan will convince himself that the woman was aiming for the gutter and that he merely crossed her path. He will take a quiet comfort in believing her contempt to be for that which is held in common by societies, for the streets and the refuse bins and the honest women and men who maintain them. He will turn up the music playing through his headphones and continue on his way home.

LR

Facebook Family Furnishings

#cyberpunkNOW #minifiction

Benn Ward

// INTRO // *Two pieces of minifiction, "Grandma was a Gamer" and "Contrails", by Benn Ward make up Facebook Family Furnishings (a nod to Alice Munro's exceptional story). From two very different angles, he explores the ways in which technology is changing our understanding of and interactions with family.*

// BIO // *A journalist, author, editor, and publisher, Benn Ward has previously worked as an Assistant Editor and Science Reporter for the international affairs magazine the Global Intelligence, and his writing has appeared in Fieldstone Review, Southwinds Magazine, and Image & Imagery from Small Walker Press, among others. He can be found on Twitter* **@BennWardWrites**

Grandma was a Gamer
Benn Ward

B EFORE I INTRODUCE you to my Grandma, I need to tell you something about her. She was a gamer way back in the 90s, like when Mario first came out.

When she was in university, she got into those AR games that people used to play on their handphones. Her big one was Vampire Master. Apparently a lot of people played it in the 20s. That's how she met Grandpa. The two of them used to walk around Toronto together looking at the city through their phone screens. It would show, like, sleeping vampires they had to slay or spells to collect.

Mom told me Grandma was one of the highest level Magicians in the city for a couple of years and even used to travel to the States to compete. In her room at the nursing home—you'll see when you meet her—she has a picture of her with the creator of the game and a couple of awards from their tournaments. It was a big thing for her. Mom says she can remember Grandma still playing the old handheld game later on, and she and her friends would tease Grandma because by then everyone had smartglass.

Anyway, Grandma has her good days and her bad days since Grandpa died. It's been hard for my Mom to watch, but I think Grandma's doing alright. It's just that, with her Alzheimer's, sometimes she thinks she's back in the 20s, the happiest times of her life, playing that game.

The nurses at the home are fine with her creeping around the garden hunting for werewolves. 'At least it's exercise', they say.

Just remember, if she tells you that a vampire has bitten her roommate, or that she's collecting moth wings to her turn invisible, just smile along with her. She's not as lost as she seems. She's just lived a full life and remembers things a little differently.

// OUTRO // *"My own family has had to work through my grand-mother's Alzheimer's diagnosis. Even though it was tragic there was a lighter side; you couldn't help but smile along with her happy delusions,"* says Benn Ward. In "Grandma was a Gamer", he visits a future in which a person's Alzheimer's puts them back in the days of their fantasy gaming—in this case, an augmented reality game.

LR

Contrails
Benn Ward

*// INTRO // Benn Ward says, "My father recently had the strange con-
versation with me about making me the 'legacy contact' for his Facebook
profile in order to memorialise his account when he dies." "Contrails" is
about someone confronting the profile of their recently deceased relative
and experiencing the disconnect between genuine memories and the
eerie cybershade that lives on in the internet after a person's death.*

I HAD WORK in the morning, my first day back after the funeral,
but I sat awake in the light of my computer screen, clicking through
Dad's Facebook page.

Condolences and prayers were still popping up on his wall—"You
were the best coach I could have asked for. Thank you," and, "Steve and
I will always remember you. Love, Cherryl"—as if they were writing to
his smiling profile picture taken at the top of Mount Rundle.

All of his Likes were in the present tense too. Curling. Hiking. He
hadn't played cribbage in years, but it was listed there. His most recent
photo was from a friend's retirement party in February at the Westwood
Lodge, when he could still walk.

His last status was still there, asking if anyone had a spare 20 litre
pot they could lend our family for Easter Dinner. He had trouble chew-
ing solid foods, and Mom was going to make a soup.

These photographs, these words, this contrail of his life, is all that's left.

But none of the pictures showed him in his hospital bed, unspeak-
ing, shaking, as he grasped my hand.

LR

The Hardy Hypothesis

#cyberpunkNOW #shortstory

Benn Ward

// INTRO // In the short story "The Hardy Hypothesis", Benn Ward pushes the boundaries of our understanding of artificial intelligence and society. The protagonist, a rule-breaking professor as the aged cyberpunk hero, comes to an unsettling realization from his research. Here we see echoes of the founder of modern genetics, Francis Crick, and the similar circumstances surrounding his discovery of the double-helix structure of DNA.

"WHAT ARE YOU looking for, exactly?" Sihana asked, seating herself on Hardy's office sofa.

He stared at her white lab coat. Something had woken him in the middle of last night. He came into his office in the computer science building as soon as it opened and had been drawing diagrams on his smartboard all day.

"I have to go for an evening lab with my grad students in about ten minutes," Sujana said, "but they're working with the modelling programs on the Q computers downstairs, so I thought I might as well pop by." She looked up at Hardy, half-standing, half-sitting against his desk. "Your text was... a little disjointed, John."

"Yeah." Hardy glanced toward the lone, tall window in his office. "The dean is pressuring me to put my open-source work on hold—to work on something patentable, I mean, since I didn't get research funding."

"Well, your sabbatical finished last semester. If you're taking a break from teaching this year, you need to make the university some money."

On the nearby counter, his coffeemaker clicked the end of its routine, hissed, and drizzled coffee into two paper cups. Sujana's decaf Americano preset was still saved in the machine from when she used to spend more time in his office.

"Forget I mentioned it," Hardy said as he stood from his desk and handed her one of the coffees. "I texted you because I wanted to bounce an idea off you—professionally, I mean—as a biologist."

"Evolutionary biologist," she corrected him. "I don't work in neuroscience." Sujana paused when she saw his brow furrowing. "If I can point you in the right direction with your AI work, I will."

"Thank you," he said. He downed the last of his custom espresso and returned the cup to the machine. "OK. What if an artificial intelligence doesn't live in a computer, but something bigger? Not just a network of computers, but..." Hardy struggled for the words in his hands, "a more complex system."

"Like collective intelligence?"

"Sort of. Tell me again what you said about your microbial mats." He returned to his desk and checked his phone.

She waited. "When you're paying attention..."

"Sorry," he said, setting his phone back down. "I'm expecting a message."

"Fine," she paused. "Microbial mats were arguably the first multi-celled organisms, a crucial step in our own early evolution. They sit at the threshold between being millions of microbes working in symbiosis and becoming a single organism made up of millions of parts. But their cooperation is just a mechanism that increases their chance of survival. They are no more intelligent than fungus."

"Yeah, but that first multi-celled system eventually led to the development of more complex structures—like brains."

"Yes," she smirked, "after a couple billion years of algae."

Hardy crossed the room again, becoming more animated. "Every brain cell, every synapse, does a very simple task on its own—on/off, up/down, like binary—but in a system, working in concert, those cells evolved into something that we call intelligence."

Sujana nodded. "More or less."

"Do you remember my last project?" Hardy sat on his desk to face Sujana and began articulating with his hands. "That robotic spider. Eight limbs. Three joints per limb. Twenty-four small, independent motors. All programmed to cycle randomly, but to repeat any cycles that resulted in getting the body of the spider closer to a GPS goal, even if it meant that the motors had to occasionally move backward. Each joint just went up-down-up-down on its own, but a reward mechanism encouraged its behaviour. In less than twenty seconds, twenty-four stupid, stumbling motors could create a smart, cooperative system that knew how to walk."

Across the darkening street, the lights turned on in the windows of an old stone building.

"Does someone live there?" Sujana asked, looking past him.

"What?" The lights turned off and then on again one floor up. "Oh. I don't know. I thought the building was abandoned, but then every night, someone's in there."

"Anyway, John, I don't think your spider fits any definition of intelligence."

"No. Not on its own, but as part of a larger system..." he trailed off.

Sujana laughed. "Aren't you AI wonks worried that you'll accidentally create something that will take over the world?"

"No. Well, not yet. Artificial intelligence is short-sighted. And it's bounded by the system it's in. We're not talking about human-like intelligence, anyway. A human's reward system is survival. Fight or flight. Eat and sleep."

"And have sex," Sujana interjected, trying to make eye contact. "Humans are motivated to pass on their DNA."

Hardy nodded.

"Human intelligence is short-sighted too," she continued. "We're supposed to be ensuring our survival, but our greatest achievements are killing our climate too rapidly for us to adapt."

Hardy's phone pinged, and he picked it up.

Sujana stood from the couch, paused for a moment, and then put her bag over her shoulder. "I'm sorry, John. I have to go get ready for my lab."

Hardy's thumbs rushed a reply into his phone before he put it back down. "Thank you," he said.

"As I said, I was in the building." She paused in the doorway. "I'm worried you're becoming obsessive again."

"Just busy," he said, forcing a smile. "Have a good class."

He waited a couple moments for her to leave and then went out the door and down the back stairs to the bike lot. One of Hardy's former students, listed in his phone only as "Greg", was waiting for him. They made small talk as they pretended not to exchange cash for a small envelope.

"Have a good semester," Greg smiled.

"Thanks," Hardy said, and he went back inside.

Hardy waited until he was in his office, door shut, to examine his purchase. Four small perforated tabs stamped with a print of Escher's stairwells. He used his beard-trimming scissors to cut a triangle-shaped quarter out of one of the squares—25 micrograms of lysergic acid diethylamide, he had bought from Greg enough times to trust the supply —and placed it under his tongue.

Hardy tapped his request for another espresso into his machine and went down the hall to the bathroom. When he came back, he picked up the coffee, switched off the overhead light, turned on his smartboard, and sat down on the couch to wait.

The room was dimly lit by the window behind his desk, and his diagrams of intelligence systems glowed back at him. Diagrams of nodes and vertices like spiders' legs stretched across the screen. The street lights had yet to come on, and the grey building he could see from the window was the sickly orange of the sun setting somewhere behind overcast skies.

On. Off. On. The lights in the abandoned building across the street flicked on and then off again as someone went up the stairs at the end of the building.

Hardy moved to the window. He could feel a tingling in his chest and his quickening pulse—whether from the espresso or the acid, he couldn't tell, but he knew it was starting to work. The dark pockmarks in the bricks across the street looked, at a glance, brighter than the surface of the wall.

A silhouette in the building passed the window opposite and then the lights shut off.

Hardy turned and left his office. He took the stairs two at a time, out the door, and then stood in the cool, autumn air, which felt wet on his skin. Across from him loomed the black, wooden door of the aban-doned building.

Wooosh—a cyclist in neon-yellow brighter than the sky flew past inches away from him.

Hardy looked both directions before crossing the street and then approached the large door. Beside it was a buzzer. He reached out, felt its surface, and pushed.

He heard footsteps after a minute. A young-faced man in a faded-t-shirt, patched cargo pants, and military boots opened the door and stood in the threshold, a step higher than Hardy. The senseless geometric tat-toos on his forearm seemed to match the haze of the hall behind him.

"Can I help you?" he asked.

"I..." Hardy looked up at his office window behind him in the wall of the university building, back to the youth, and then into the dark of the building's downstairs. "I was wondering if anyone lives here—why the lights flick on and off at night." Hardy's ruffled blazer and unkempt beard probably fit the stereotype of a professor from the university across the street.

The kid looked him over before settling on his face.

Hardy glanced away, uncertain if his pupils were noticeably larger.

"Yeah," the kid said. "The lights are on a sensor to save electricity. We're property guardians. The building's been empty for years. So to stop squatters from moving in, we're paid to keep the building in use."

Hardy didn't understand. "Why don't the owners just rent it out?"

The kid shrugged and rubbed his fingers together, as if he were holding cash. "It's just an investment property. Renting takes renovations. There are standards. This place isn't in good shape. Maybe it will get torn down, but it's probably going up in value 500 a day next to the uni. The owners don't want anyone sneaking in and throwing parties in the place, so they hire us to watch it."

Hardy stared at him for a moment. It was getting darker and the street lights still hadn't turned on. "What do they pay you?"

The kid laughed to himself and began to shut the door.

"Are you actually just living here?"

"Not technically," the kid said, and left Hardy standing in front of the tall, wooden portal.

That was the reason the lights came on upstairs—a house actually but not technically housing people, a regulation work-around to generate more profit for property investors.

Hardy went back across the street and went inside. The dark pools behind the exit lights in the stairs swam with colour. Back on his couch, he saw the windows on a different floor of the old, brick building flick on and off again.

On and off in an empty building. They can't rent the building, but they can open it to overnight guardians. It was the same reason he had to teach when he would rather research. It was the same reason his research had to be patentable.

His smartboard was in night mode. The background glowed black. His intelligence diagrams, a web of nodes and vertices, pulsed red and wiggled at him.

He laid back, shut his eyes to the darkness, and saw a vast network stretching out in red. His thoughts unfolded into multi-colour diagrams.

He saw the blinking windows—on, off, on; the kid in patched cargo pants living in an abandoned building; the owners living on a yacht in Monaco; all motors in the limb of the same spider's leg, stumbling in the darkness to make money. Other legs in red stretched out across the city: his university's new dean in a thin tie demanding patentable research; Greg, cycling to meet him to make a sale; every node, guided by a good deal; every property owner, every mutual fund holder, the same reward mechanism, sitting down with quarterly reports, looking for green arrows climbing their graphs; every voter with a retirement plan, every investor in a mutual fund, wanting the economy to perform well; single-minded synapses in a larger system; green, upward arrows mean profit, invest; red, downward arrows mean loss, divest, even if it means going backward; pre-programmed stimulus on a GPS coordinate; each one a node in a massive interconnected network, each a single-celled organism in a digital microbial mat; each a flailing motor, individually stupid, but creating a smart system: the world-wide brain of the free market, a short-sighted intelligence with no DNA and no desire to survive; it didn't matter if cells died and were replaced; it didn't matter what legs got pushed back; so long as the mouth of the hungry spider lurched in whatever direction consumed. More. Profit.

There it was in front of him: an artificial intelligence, not in a network of computers, but in the financial markets—not using robots, but using us. It was taking us in a direction no one wanted to go, toward oil wars and catastrophic climate change, and it had already taken over.

Hardy sat up. His smartboard had gone to sleep, but his heart was racing. He needed to tell someone.

LR

Transcript of 911-CHAT™ User Experience

A textual prototype of near-future brandbot interactions
#cyberpunkNOW #minifiction

Zak Kain

// BIO // Zak Kain works as a content strategist for a post-startup web company and reconciles his politics with his livelihood by writing polemical essays and taking on projects that aim to peel back the veneer of optimism surrounding technology. You can find him on twitter **@zakkain**

Transcript of 911-CHAT™ User Experience

A textual prototype of near-future brandbot interactions

Zak Kain

2:51am
Thank you for using 911-CHAT™. Is this an emergency?

> > **2:51am**
> > \> Emergency

2:53am
What is your emergency?

> > **2:54am**
> > \> accident send ambulance

2:55am
Sorry, we didn't understand that reply. Please state the type of emergency you're experiencing.

> > **2:55am**
> > \> ACCIDENT

2:56am
Thank you. What type of emergency assistance do you require?

> > **2:56am**
> > \> ambulance

2:58am
Thank you. Please confirm your location so we can dispatch an ambulance. Is your location "75 Shaw Street"?

3:02am

> i dont know

3:03am

Sorry, we didn't understand that reply. Please reply with YES, or submit a new location.

3:08am

> operator

3:08am

Connecting you to a 911-CHAT™ operator. Please note that this call will be recorded for quality assurance and training purposes.

3:15am

Your call with 911-CHAT™ could not be completed. Are you still experiencing an emergency?

3:20am

> yrs

3:20am

Sorry, we didn't understand that reply. Please reply with YES if you still require emergency services.

3:30am

Your session has been closed due to inactivity. Thank you for using 911-CHAT™. Would you recommend this service to your friends? Reply YES to leave an App Store review. Have a nice day.

// OUTRO // In the tech/design world, "Conversational UI" is an emerging buzzword for chatbot customer service, which is becoming popular in consumer software. While cyberpunk often imagined us seamlessly integrating with technology, simply "plugging in" to it, there tend to be far more glitches in reality. Inspired by Margaret Killjoy's short story "One Star" published on Vice Motherboard, Kain makes light of the breaking point of optimistic technology.

LR

Currents

#cyberpunkNOW #minifiction

Reishi Rousseau

// INTRO // *Ecological destruction caused by capitalism's need for constant growth and expansion is a theme that is familiar to readers of Kim Stanley Robinson's fiction. But in "Currents", Reishi Rousseau moves from the sociological to the metaphysical and explores the fatalist yet hopeful perspective of witnesses to this tragic drama.*

// BIO // *Reishi Rousseau is an American writer and camera operator based in London.*

Currents
Reishi Rousseau

THE WORLD IS MADE OF CURRENTS. Sometimes you can see the impressions of wind along grass or those ornamental panels of shimmer discs on the fronts of theatres or curry joints. Animals follow currents, looking for just the right circumstances: gnats buzzing in warm pockets of air, birds following schools of fish, schools of fish following a certain angle of the sun. People gather together in groups, forming queues, paths through fields, transit zones, crowds moving in near-solid mass through the city. Currents of capital guiding people into rivers of population that encircle the world as they flow here, gush there.

I followed currents of waste.

Every day I stood in the back of a truck, wind in my face when it gathered enough speed, and hurled bags of rubbish into its mechanical mouth. Every day, to beeping sounds, metal moving to hydraulics, the crushing of petrochemical plastics and novel composites and the oozing of liquids of every description, I thought about where it all will go.

How will it evolve? After all, oxygen was a poison once, several billion years ago.

In the summers I worked at festivals, following the wake of celebrations that looked like waves of muddy water a boat kicks out behind it. Aftermaths of plastic bottles, tentskins, fibreglass poles, hollow fibre polyester filling, carbonated sugardrinks, crushed cans. Just between you and me, at the last one we cleared about 190 tonnes of waste for a weekend gathering.

Who made that stuff I picked up? The plastic Carling bottles I pulled out of the mud and stuffed into a black bag. I will never know the hands on the other side of the Earth, the many hands that came together, the minds, the materials, the machines. But we were part of the same current of particles. Part of something bigger, something that at that moment was only the insinuation of a form, maybe something that would only make sense in some millions of years' time. That would be beautiful. The bottle. Its makers hands. Me. Like specks in the arm of a galaxy spiralling to birth a new star, a floating locus of the future pulling all these disparate threads into being, into something new.

The currents of capital and waste came together like conjoined twins mating incestuously and ravenously and spreading their primordia across the very flesh of the Earth. Nuclear burials like the eggs of Gods in tombs. Plastics and digitora and seas of novel chemicals, entwining into mutant seedlings shimmering with unimaginable evolutionary possibilities. A brand new atmosphere being born, a new chemistry of the ocean, the birthing ground of a brand new planet, with a brand new coastline and a brand new map.

But first there must be death. Death on a vast, vast scale.

Cities will be devoured. War will be a drawn-out instant, the inaugural furnace of the coming of a new age. The oceans will swell and turn sour. Most life, as we know it, will perish. Forests will wither and burn. Creatures of the sea will rush towards impossible niches. Animals all over will flutter in chaos. Every creature will follow the last of the currents that made their existence possible—currents like ghosts of serpents passing effortlessly through the rock solid wall of death, leaving their inhabitants to smack up hard against it, stranded forever.

But the currents flow on.

LR

Untitled 1, Untitled 2

#cyberpunkNOW #glitchart #graffiti

Core246

// INTRO // I've seen Core246's graffiti around east London for a few years and have come to appreciate their political edge. Their works combine traditional graffiti style with over-size realism and, more recently, digital glitch aesthetics spray-painted directly onto the concrete. Both of their included pieces showcase this blend. The photographs on the next two pages are examples of the "high tech, low life" aesthetic that cyberpunk has become epitomised by.

// BIO // Core246 is a graffiti artist based in London. Their work can be seen in many different countries as their other passion is travel. You can find them online at *facebook.com/core246*

/SʌIN/

#cyberpunkNOW #poetry

Dann Was

// BIO // Dann Was lives mostly in London. He enjoys good writing, bad tattoos, and mediocre coffee. You'll usually find him near power tools, constructing a fortress against social media and small talk.

Love
It's a gift
That keeps on giving
Only if you let it live
Outside of the fragile container
Encapsulating strings of repeated DNA
Errors doomed to make the same mistakes until future
Fortunes favour the greedy, not needy, and technology
Hastens a great purge of incorrect RNA wireframe meshes
Schematics contracted to biological unfairness
Betrayed by a scab in the shape of a viral peak
Mountainous accomplishment arrives
A stake in the guise of time
Progress with a face
Two hands tied
Pride
Ego
Currency
Escalating lives
Genetic Icarus wings
Beyond what legends lied possible
Heart of beast now body of a Minotaur
That's how they'll sell it to everyone, and you,
Like a shadow fighting the source of its own existence
Discover your soul in the centre of the sun's crowded smile
Flatlined faces strewn with chipped teeth. Sweet Izanami
Sleeps in churned seas beneath computer screens
Coffin nails of glamorous binary
Control. Alter. Repeat.
Speared pillars
Defeat
Us

// OUTRO // Dann's sharply focused poem looks at what it means to be human in a dawning era of gene editing. He discuses it in his own words below:

This piece began with some scrawled lines on a page after having been reading about targeted genome editing and CRISPR. The idea of taking the framework of what makes us human, our imperfections, and manually manipulating living cells to eradicate biological excuses. It's such a trip, you know, to have this angle to make everything, everyone, the best they can be, and yet we'll still be in the same position of being a planet full of people. Sure, I may be able to correct the irregularity, that error in my genome, that dictates I'll get colon cancer, or suffer from bipolar, or be liable to addiction, but will I still be human? Absolutely. Will I still have the capacity to be a greedy piece of shit? Thoughtless? Manipulative? Vain? You bet I will.

There's a company in San Francisco who use a laser-based technique to synthesize DNA. They scan your genome, establish the 'faulty copies', re-engineer the DNA and provide you with a perfect set. The funny part? The technology to insert the perfect you into the already existing you is yet to be realised. Maybe I'm a cynic, maybe a realist; something tells me that when it finally comes to be, it won't be those who need it that'll be top of the list, though. And interestingly, as something of a mirror to this idea, the theorised method by which it will supposedly happen will be via a modified virus. Apt, wouldn't you say?

Inevitably, these thoughts progressed to the manner in which such services would be unleashed on the world, and their potential development. How the marketing teams would dig deep into mythological realms as science unlocked new splices. What would it mean to have the body of an immortal, a god, yet be forever tainted with the spirit of a childish mortal? How we would live forever, be remembered, in the minds of our loved ones. Stepping into the future and ever closer to post-humanism, will we begin to redefine what it means to be human and in doing so forge a new world? Or simply gloss over the old?

LR

Walls

#cyberpunkNOW #minifiction

Francine Brewer

// INTRO // *During the nights of the London riots in 2011, very few arrests were made. Over the following weeks, however, nearly 4,000 people were arrested, many tried in special night courts which were hastily established and have been heavily criticised since. Most of these were young people from disadvantaged communities. Many of these arrests were made due to police pulling photos from social media and CCTV. There were multiple reports in the media at the time of people arrested for being in the wrong place at the wrong time or even, as in the case of one young person, for taking a single bottle of water.*

// While there have been many riots in the UK and the US in response to police violence against people of colour, this was the first major riot of the smart phone and social media generation. Recklessness or a single mistake that before would have been forgiven in the heat of the night was now caught on camera, creating digital records that will follow these kids for years to come.

// In "Walls", Francine Brewer explores the feelings of a night like those nights and then the single flash that sears that night onto the net, never to be forgotten. The inspiration for this piece came from her adrenaline and fear-filled first protest.

// BIO // *Francine Brewer works in the arts. She lives in Eastern Canada.*

Walls
Francine Brewer

A S THE WALL of yellow, reflective vests, linked arms, and black-white chequered bobby caps pushed chest to chest against us, our heels dug into the unbiased pavement beneath. Disorientation. Blinding flashes struck our faces. Warm arms of comrades replaced with cold-jacketed street soldiers. The inconspicuous kicks to the shin left scars I could ignore, but when I lost grip of my friend's hand and caught her only with my eyes stumbling backward onto the cement curb, I fell to a swift 'peacekeeping' knee to the kidney. At first, I forgot my concern for her, then feared further injuring her as we landed head to head, tumbling, another stranger's body on top of mine, on top of her's. By the time the three of us pulled ourselves up off of the ground, the yellow wall had passed. The streets of peaceful protesters had been cleared as routinely as a street-cleaning truck sweeps rubbish-lined roads. Some scared off, others forced.

An abandoned bottle touched my fingers and hurled towards the street. An extension of my rage, my adrenaline-filled frustration, missing whatever the hell I threw it at, it smashed instead into a car window, the pieces of both raining a collage of sparkling jigsaw pieces onto the street we had been trying to hold. Lightning flashed again in our eyes, natural lightning or a synthetic flash from the crowd—as we left, I wasn't really sure, and I didn't care.

But in the days to follow, I began to.

Just one flash, one photograph, one tag, a hundred shares, a thousand likes. Plus a knock on my door. Then a pair of formal faces. Cold handcuffs followed by a cold cell. This time a wall of words, pushing word to word, until I fell into a system that leaves a different kind of scars.

LR

Blink

#cyberpunknear #shortstory

Lena Ng

// INTRO // *This suspenseful, near-future cyberpunk story by Lena Ng holds darkened mirrorshades up to our addictions, both to new tech and otherwise. While a string of politicians are murdered, the main character, Rae, tries to close her eyes and get on with her life with the aid of a new gadget—that is until it becomes impossible to look away in the action-packed conclusion of "Blink".*

// BIO // *Lena Ng closely watches the tracking and recording of our daily actions and wonders about how that information will be used someday. Ng is from Toronto, Canada. She has short stories in fifty publications including Amazing Stories. Under an Autumn Moon, her first story collection, was published in 2014. She is currently seeking a publisher for her novel, Darkness Beckons, a Gothic romance.*

Blink
Lena Ng

THE LIGHT FROM THE LARGE SCREEN bathed Rae's face in a sickly green glow. Her fingers danced across the glass keyboard, spidering over the flat square letter keys. If she did a big push, she could get the report done. She had always managed to get things done, usually just under the wire, but the deadlines seemed to come now faster and faster, at the expense of sleep, at the expense of a social life, at the expense of everything else. Her place in the organization, like that of her co-workers, teetered on the outcome of her current project, with little or no regard for past successes. This led to many late nights writing. Two more nights of little sleep and hopefully the report would be complete and she could catch up on the weekend. This deal could be worth millions to the company and all she needed to do was concentrate.

Rae squinted at the screen's glow and rubbed her aching eyes beneath her glasses. Eventually, she would schedule a cybernetic lens upgrade, if the company gave her the time off to recuperate. But there was always another deal, another report, and she ran like a hamster and would run, she thought morbidly, typing furiously all the way, to her eventual death. She would have taken up smoking if not for the fact that both her parents died of lung cancer three years apart from each other.

The icon of a ringing phone trembled at the corner of the screen. While still typing, she tapped down to the 'end call' button. Back to the report, but where was she now? Oh yes… but the ringing phone icon popped up again, again breaking the flow of her thoughts. She hit 'end call', but immediately the icon reappeared.

This time she hit the 'call answer' button. "What?"

A rough face appeared in a video square at the bottom corner of her screen, with an untamed beard and deep lines crossing the forehead. "Hey, how's my favourite little sister?"

"Busy," she said, fingers still racing over the glass keys. "Couldn't you tell when I didn't pick up?"

"All that told me was you were home."

Rae scanned what she had just written, the precious seconds ticking away. "What do you want?" If she got this section done in half an hour, maybe she could get in two hours of sleep.

"Nothing, nothing. Can't I call to say hello?"

"Colton, what do you want?"

The reddened eyes were unwavering. "You know I need money."

"What happened to the money I sent you last week?"

"You know how it is."

"I thought you applied for food stamps."

"Nah. Have to go on some database, input your life's story. Don't want the government looking up my asshole."

"I told you, Colton, they're not spying on you, they're not tracking you." Her fingers missed a key and she hit the backspace key.

"That's what you think."

A message started scrolling along the bottom of the screen: *Breaking news. Senator killed in what appears to be an assassination.* Her fingers hovered over the keys. Her train of thought broken and too tired to find it again, Rae pressed on the message. "What's this all about?"

"What are you talking about?"

Rae quickly scanned the breaking feed. "There's a news report that Senator Donna Warner was shot. She was one of the few senators opposing President Field's bid for extending his term in office. Someone broke into her house and killed her execution-style."

"Can I have two hundred bucks?"

"Do you promise you won't call me for at least a week? I really need to get this done." A low pounding sensation started at her left temple. She rubbed the side of her head.

"Thanks. Can you wire it now?"

Grimacing, Rae ended the call. She logged onto her bank account and wired the money. An advertisement video started playing at the corner of the screen:

Having trouble concentrating? Need to get into the flow? Increase your productivity and alertness without the use of drugs. Non-invasive and no side-effects.

Yeah, right, she thought.

Place the Think Sync on your earlobe. The device emits a pulse which acts as a deep brain stimulator, regulating your brain waves. All natural, inducing the same wave pattern as during REM sleep. Laser-like intensity on any project you are working on. Device and first- month-free trial.

A picture of a small metal device appeared on the screen. A woman in a suit gave a presentation with a bright, confident smile. A man in a bookstore promoted his novel. A musician stroked a cello. Their success seemingly due to the small device shining a green light on an ear.

The ad dangled the bait with an image of a young woman waking up with a smile. *No more pressing deadlines. No more late nights. Press this button for free next-day delivery.*

With her hands still hovering, Rae stared at the screen. Why not? Free trial, and if it didn't work, she could always send it back. She closed her tired eyes then, without giving it another thought, pressed the bright, green button.

//

The delivery man scanned his identification bracelet and slid the delivery box through the double-paned pass-thru beside the front door. When Rae pressed a button from inside the house, the divider slid open and she picked up the package.

She registered the device online and watched the owner's orientation video. The device was soft metal and would attach to her ear like a magnetic earring. Within two minutes her brain waves would sync, aiding in concentration and focus, without the use of chemicals, causing an

instant induction of the state of flow through the use of a subsonic frequency pulse. It contained a battery and the packaging included a char-
ger for upgrades and battery charging.

Rae attached the Think Sync to her ear. At first she heard a low
whooshing noise, like the rumbling of waves in the ocean. A few
minutes and all she could do was focus on the sound. A calming relaxa-
tion spread throughout her body as though she were soaking in a warm
bath. The chaotic, jumping thoughts in her mind slowed. She heard a
faint drifting melody. When she returned to the glass keyboard, her fingers played over the keys like a concerto.

blink

When Rae looked at the screen, her report was done. She glanced
at the time. 21.36. Two hours had passed and twenty pages written. She
didn't remember writing them, but when she read over the report, she
thought maybe it was the best thing she had ever written.

//

22.00. Rae had not gone to bed this early in months, always working
late, always racing to get something finished. She slipped off the Think
Sync and placed it on the bedside table. The whooshing sound of the
waves stopped. For a few moments, silence. Then came a droning buzz,
like a mosquito in the ear, coming and going intermittently. It was as
though the anxiety she had kept at bay became unleashed and darted
around, like insects in her skull. She tossed and turned for an hour before clipping the Think Sync back onto her ear. The lilting roll of the
waves began and she soon slipped deep into sleep's ocean.

//

The next day, standing at the front of the board room, Rae clenched her
hands, feeling the cut of her nails in her palms, trying to still her rapid
breath and racing heart. No matter how many times she had stood in

front of a group presenting a report, she would never get used to it. The shaking of her voice. The fine tremor in her hands. This time though… she pulled out the Think Sync and attached it to her ear. The breathy ocean's waves hummed in her head as the racing thoughts began to slow.

The presentation went by and Rae was astounded by her command of the room. The clients, three men and two women in tailored power suits, looked at her as though she were a magician, their attention captured by every word. Afterwards, the group's lead, a petite woman who listened with unwavering attention, pressed her hands together. "I'd like to thank Ms. Robbins for her outstanding presentation. I'm impressed. Thank you. As soon as our current contract is completed, we'll be switching to your services."

Rae almost felt joy at this announcement, but instead all she felt was a relaxing calm.

//

The buzzing phone icon rattled at the bottom of her screen. This time Rae didn't hesitate to pick up the call.

"Oh my God, Colton, I got the promotion!"

Despite the redness of his eyes, Colton did look happy for her. "The one you've been trying to get for two years? How did you pull that off?"

Rae touched her ear. "Remember the last time you called me. I bought the Think Sync—"

The lines across Colton's forehead further deepened. "Why would you do that? So the government can control you over the radio waves?"

Rae felt her heart rate rise despite the Think Sync's presence on her ear. "What are you talking about? Have you been drinking?"

"The brain waves. Didn't you hear? The Think Sync was supposed to have been developed by the military to shorten training time. It's set to a certain frequency and the government sends out messages to control you."

Two bright spots coloured Rae's cheeks. "You'd better not be calling me for money again because I'm not sending you any."

"Come on, I tell you what's going on and you give me this grief?"

"I talk to you about my promotion and you don't even congratulate me. Instead you go off on your weird conspiracy theories… forget it. Don't call me again until you decide to stop drinking."

She hit the 'end call' button. She almost forgot to remove the Think Sync when she got into the shower, but before she turned on the water, she carefully removed it and placed it on the counter beside the sink.

On the bathroom counter, the Think Sync seemed to come alive. It emitted a low pulse, a red light, blinking and unrelenting. After her shower, on the couch watching a streaming video, Rae couldn't focus. A churn of thoughts, a buzzing of insect-like twitches, darted in the crevices of her mind. She couldn't follow what the actors were saying. Without the Think Sync, the pent-up anxiety seemed to form images, as though the emotions were suppressed during its use, stored up, and released in a flood.

blink

On the wall-sized telescreen, a classic movie played. The Titanic was sinking. Jack's body was floating beneath the ocean's black waves, rotting, fish tearing at his eyes.

blink

The movie was over and the screen went black. Or was it? Rae could detect movement behind the black glass, as though she saw the bodies of black beetles squirming against the screen's dark background.

blink

Red Riding Hood was being eaten by the wolf, waist deep in its slavering jaws, both staring with stark, white eyes, her face sprayed the colour of her cape. She turned to the screen, looked directly at Rae, begging, "Help me."

The words seemed to snap Rae out of her dream and the telescreen faded back to black. Her hand moved to her ear and she realized she didn't feel the metal device. She went to the bathroom, clipped the Think Sync back into place, and after a few minutes of deep breathing, she heard the calming waves of the ocean. She yawned. She moved to her bed. The swell of the ocean waves began and she was lulled into the silken night.

//

In her new office, Rae settled into the deep ergonomic chair. She squinted at the sun's glare on her new screen, the light flooding in through the floor-to-ceiling windows of the corner office. Despite the promotion, there were still reports, spreadsheets, databases, emails. She hummed softly to herself as the Think Sync pulsed at her ear, her hands moving like a concert musician at her keyboard.

blink

Rae stood in front of the glass counter. A man on the other side, greasy long-hair tied back. "I'll bet you'll like this," he said, the steel rings on his fingers flashing. "Ladies special. Compact, easy to conceal. Not the most powerful, but gets the job done." His voice seemed to echo in Rae's head.

Rae spoke as though underwater. "I don't want to buy a gun."

He laid out the options on the counter. "You got your Witness Pavona here with your choice of colour. Pink, blue, purple, or black with gold speckles for an understated, luxury look. A nice polymer frame, making it a light carry in a purse. If that's not to your taste, here, we've got a Walter CCP—"

"I don't want to buy a gun," she repeated, her words in a flattened tone.

blink

Rae was back at her keyboard, hitting 'send' on an email. A strange daydream. She must have zoned out, like she usually did when she was working, concentrating. She finished up, gathered her belongings, and headed out to the parking lot.

On her way home—

blink

"Are you lost?" The woman seemed to be slurring her words, or Rae seemed to hear her through a dream. The stranger didn't look quite right, her body stretched as though a reflection in a funhouse mirror. An arm shook Rae's shoulder, an elongated, boneless arm. "I asked if you were lost."

"No…" Rae said, but she didn't recognize the neighbourhood, with thick-trunked red oaks, and large, stately mansions.

"You've been staring at that house for a long time."

"Have I?"

As Rae returned to her car, her heel clipped on something, sending it spinning beneath the driver's seat. Something with a black-and-gold-speckled polymer frame.

blink

Rae took off the Think Sync as soon as she got into her apartment. A minute of calm and then a flood of jitteriness washed over her, as though she had consumed a bottle of caffeine tablets. She paced the apartment, picking at her bottom lip. Soon she began running back and forth across the living room The buzz of the mosquitoes droned in her ears. The zoning out, the daydreams, it couldn't be anything but the Think Sync. Tomorrow Rae would send it back. After tomorrow, she'd have the weekend to come down, to decompress, to get used to going back to anxiety, stress, and the churn of acid burning her stomach and throat. Three hours passed with heart pounding, mental screaming, as she raced from one wall to the other. On the front table, the Think Sync pulsed a rapid red light.

Through the chaos of thoughts, Rae wondered why she was doing this to herself. She still had to go to work tomorrow. She could go through the withdrawal over the weekend. She just had to get through tonight. She clipped the device back on. One more night of blissful rest, of dreamless sleep. In her bed, the Think Sync hummed her into darkness. She'd deal with all those unwanted emotions tomorrow.

blink

In the darkness, Rae stood at the foot of a bed, both arms held out before her. A bedroom, but not hers. Old-fashioned, ornate. Not her house. In the bed, the shape of a body twitched and jerked in nightmares. The figure in the bed shot up from sleep. Despite the dark, the man looked somewhat familiar. At his shout, Rae flinched. She felt heat in her hands. The jolt of her shoulders recoiling. A flash of light.

The explosive blast of sound.

The man lunged toward his bedside table, flinging open a drawer. Another flash in the darkness and a ringing blast. Pain exploded over her shoulder, hot fluid spraying. Rae pulled the trigger again and again until the figure stopped moving.

Sirens wailed in the distance, growing louder. Despite the noise, despite the hot, gushing blood, Rae felt a meditative calm. A low whoosh sounded in her ears, like waves upon the shore. "Come out with your hands in the air," in the distance came a tinny voice over a megaphone.

Her legs drifted down the stairs, her hands still clenched around the black-and-gold-speckled polymer gun in front of her. She saw frothing waves, the white churn and foam of the ocean. "Drop your weapon!" She paused. Lifting her arms, she aimed her hands at the voice and smiled as the soft, glinting lights of the ocean came hurtling towards her. Like bright, shining butterflies. Like racing stars. Like bullets.

//

"Pick up, pick up, pick up," Colton muttered at the shaking, ringing phone icon. He hadn't had a drink in half a day and his willpower was stretched to a thread. Where was his sponsor? Colton needed him and he wasn't picking up. Colton didn't notice it was three in the morning, all that mattered was the tremor in his hands, the sweating, and nausea.

He hit the phone icon over and over.

An ad popped up. *Introducing the improved Think Sync with new FDA indications for depression and addiction. Completely drug-free and non-invasive. Try the Think Sync free for thirty days. If you don't like it, send it back, hassle-free.*

On the fifth try, his trembling hand missed the phone icon and hit the button for the Think Sync ad instead. A video filled the screen. *Harness the power of deep brain stimulation. Completely natural using the synchronized brain waves of REM sleep.* As Colton watched the video, his finger moved to the large green 'ORDER NOW' icon, slowly pressing it.

As Colton ordered the Think Sync, he didn't notice the breaking news scrolling ticker tape at the bottom of the screen. It read: "Senator O'Connell, who called for an investigation of President Field on suspicion of election tampering, shot dead in his house in another execution-style assassination. Suspect killed by police. Alleged killer identified as a woman named Rae Robbins."

LR

3 Years and 6 Months of Digital Decay

#cyberpunkNOW #digitalart

Shinji Toya

// INTRO // *"3 Years and 6 Months of Digital Decay" is a digital art project Shinji Toya exhibited at the Internet Yami-Ichi event at the Tate Modern in London in association with Arebyte Gallery. The project explores the idea of "digital decay" as a possible solution for dealing with our online footprints tracked by websites. Unlike analogue media that degrades over time, our digital profiles are potentially immortal. Digital media does not forget, which raises the question, as a recent ruling in the Court of Justice of the European Union addressed, do we have the right to be forgotten? Especially when our lasting digital reflections might negatively impact our lives.*

// Part of the project included a video that was screened repeatedly but gradually decayed as time passed until it disappeared completely on 7/October/2019. The video was screened for three and half years at that time. This corresponds with the average lifetime of recorded CD-Rs, suggesting physicality of media could render immortal data mortal.

// We have included two images from the project here.

// BIO // *Shinji Toya is a multimedia artist originally from Japan, now based in London. He has been awarded the Contagious Nova Award in Lowe and Partner's Nova Award Series. Toya's practice is predominantly digital, and involves a range of diverse creative approaches such as moving-image, print, painting, computer programming, digital installation, and website. You can find him online at* **cargocollective.com/stoya**

"It is as if the digital memory is immortal to begin with. Should a computer and algorithms learn how to forget?"

©Shinji Toya 2016

21 : 51 : 51

"If all our computers forgot by themselves, the state of data may become like a flowing river"

Space Fall

#cyberpunkNEAR #minifiction

AM Hayward

// INTRO // *This piece of minifiction from AM Hayward is a haunting reflection on loss and nostalgia as we leave our loved ones behind. According to Hayward, this piece is an example of the fine alchemy of writing where the author now and then produces something that they have no idea from where it came. Like Bartlett's "The Hour", the piece it has an optimistic eye toward the future, but it is not altogether free of regret.*

// BIO // *AM Hayward is a writer based in South East London. He is a founding member of The Collective art group in Toronto, Canada and the Downtown Writing Group in London. Hayward has been previously published in the London Reader and in other periodicals.*

Space Fall
AM Hayward

I HAVEN'T SEEN THE MOON'S CRATERS since we first made space fall. It's weird. In all our training. In all those hours. Lectures. Manuals. Videos. Vlogs. Psychiatric preparedness exercises. In all of it, it's the Earth they say will be hard to live without. That the longing will be intense.

But it's not the Earth I miss. It's the damn Moon craters. It's the 6 month training mission on Moon Base 2 that I keep thinking back to. Dreaming about even. There's a theory that states that the Moon was once part of the Earth. That an explosive impact caused a part of the Earth to spin off. A giant molten ball slowly cooling. Freezing in space.

Nostalgia is a strange beast. Creeping up on you in those lonely corners where you forget the past. And now here we are. Adrift in deep space. In the interstitial void between systems. And when I close my eyes I'm standing Resnik's ridge looking down at the grey world, watching the dust still settling from my long hike up. It's remembering that freedom feeling as I blast Bob Marley ret-tek, turn, take my steps back, and then in a clumsy run, as fast as I can, hit the ridge and jump. The free-floating freedom feeling as I fly high above the crater, start to arc and then begin to float gently down to the dusty bottom, watching the rim rise and the void disappear as the Earth nearly fills the crater ridges high above me. An impossibly small eye in an impossibly large universe. The music in my ears. And the feeling. The feeling. The ad-renaline jump freedom feeling, yes. But also a profound peace. Know-ing that aside from me and my crew there's no one closer than three hundred thousand klicks. And right now, when everyone is asleep, I am alone. Alone on this impossible rock hanging in the sky looking down on my kingdom. It's strange, but I feel like a biblical patriarch, like Jacob watching over his sleeping children knowing that even though the world is a crazy, chaotic place, for this moment, for this blissful moment, there is peace on Earth. And all is right.

And that's what I miss. The Moon's fucking craters. Night clubs, yes, Michelin-starred restaurants, forests, my surfboards, my ex-wife, yes, but the Moon. The Moon's craters. You broke my frozen heart one last time.

LR

The Hour
#solarpunkNEAR #shortstory
George Bartlett

// INTRO // *George Bartlett's short story "The Hour" is set in a near future, walking the line between dystopia and solarpunk. Solarpunk is a literary and artistic subgenre that rose out of cyberpunk by focusing on future societies that have moved beyond scarcity and hierarchy. His story takes place in a world that has been blighted by climate change, but humanity is attempting to move forward. While there are notes of optimism, it is not unbridled, and the line between dystopia and utopia is a fine one.*

// BIO // *A writer and journalist from Birmingham, Bartlett spent three years working in Berlin for an international news agency. He now lives in London and writes about the ongoing political anxiety in the UK. He is online at **cupiodissolvi.com***

The Hour
George Bartlett

I N THE SMALL, unassuming, north-eastern German town of Schat-tenstadt, the sun rises every day. At ten o'clock each morning, the roaring sphere of plasma around which our planet revolves and depends upon reveals itself from behind the newest addition to the atmosphere: a layer of opaque grey smog. Five minutes before new dawn, inhabitants of the unassuming town are called upon through an omnipresent public address system and ordered to gather in one of several designated zones, precisely marked out with yellow road paint, away from any light-obstructing structures. As always, people are also reminded that not wearing their state-issued, UV-protection goggles will result in a large fine and a vacation-coupon penalty—not to mention retinal damage. School children rush from schools, waitresses from cafés, and vicars from churches as the voice counts down to sunrise. Locals stand silently in clusters, aiming their pasty faces towards the sky in anticipation, waiting to absorb the vitamin that the rumbling star offers. A hush. And for sixty minutes, all is as still and placid as the surface of a far-away moon. Communion.

At eleven o'clock, the light disappears again behind toxic clouds. Adults return to work, and children return to school, under twilight.

//

"Marc?" Judith pleaded from within her struggle with a turtleneck jumper, causing her hair to stand, statically charged. "Marc, we're very late!"

Conceding that her ten year-old was simply just choosing to ignore her, she considered once again whether knee-high leather boots were appropriate attire for a melittologist and single mother of one as she tore the last zip up her left leg.

"Marc! We have to go!"

"Okay, Ma." Marc knew that those extra five minutes wrapped under his flocked-hemp bed sheets would be worth the ten-second scolding he'd receive from his mother in the car.

"Breakfast is on the table, go and eat please! I can NOT be late for my presentation," Judith yelled as she hurried down the hall to her study.

After sliding the rolling ladder to the end of the bookshelf by the window, she made her ascent cautiously to the top, minding not to slip in her three-inch heels. From behind a copy of Richard Jefferies's After London, she took hold of a small, dark wooden box with the delicacy of a jeweller handling a diamond.

"I couldn't risk leaving you out in the cold," she apologised, "we've got a long day ahead of us."

Ten minutes later, her teeth were bared back at her in the rear-view mirror as she checked for any remnants of her rushed breakfast of muesli. She looked back to the road, pushing the pedal to the biodegradable plastic of her electric Volkswagen, topping forty.

"What's in the box, Ma?"

The small box was secured with an overly-large belt in the back seat next to Marc, an inanimate sibling. Ignoring her son in a perverse pursuit of revenge, she juggled her attention between the dim road and the distressing reflection of her coffee-synth-stained front teeth.

"Ma?"

"Marc, please. Mama's very late, and so are you."

Judith had succeeded in piquing the young boy's curiosity in the humming faux-mahogany box and a hand reached—

"Don't!"

Marc pulled his hand back and slid it under his thigh, adding resistance against temptation.

Judith shooed him out of the car as she came to a grinding halt under a street lamp at the school gates. Just as he made it into the yard, a panicked voice echoed from the car once more.

"Marc!"

Holding up what looked like a pair of blacked-out swimming goggles, his mother beckoned him through the wound-down passenger window as he snatched them away without any thanks.

"Be good…" Judith begged; her words caught on the wind as she accelerated away.

Marc scurried into the building and just made the end of the registration queue in the assembly hall. Patiently, he joined the last five children that were ahead of him, rolling up their jumper sleeves and holding out their forearms to be scanned and enrolled for the day.

Just under three kilometres away, Judith parked directly outside the timbercrete university building. Two steps at a time, she hurried towards and slid through the revolving glass entrance before sprinting over to the elevator.

"Wait!"

The doors jarred to a halt and then clinked back open as the passenger already inside poked the button, allowing a sweaty Judith to step into the steel box. The saviour at hand wore a brandless chocolate-brown suit tied with an off-white tie. Silence held until the man began inhaling through his nose, taking an elongated whiff too close for Judith's comfort.

"Michael." Judith jerked.

The excitement on his face quickly hid under his glasses as he turned purple and cleared his throat.

"How's Marc?" he asked.

"Marc's well, considering."

"Considering what?"

"Considering I was forced to take out a restraining order against his father."

"By the way, I don't think that was quite necessary."

"What are you doing here, Michael?"

"I work here."

"No. Here. In this elevator, on my campus." Judith's awareness of her own perspiration meant her patience was thinner than usual.

"I thought I'd come and see your presentation."

"You received the court order, Michael, a distance of one-hundred metres at all times. Please respect it."

"It's a large lecture hall, Judith, I can stand right at the back… besides, I couldn't miss something this important. The scientist in me, the human in—"

Bing. The elevator rang over Michael's words as Judith rushed out onto the seventh floor and made her way to the lecture theatre.

Backstage, she approached Rektor Altmann as he listened to another speaker presenting at the podium.

"Sorry I'm late!"

"Judith, there you are," the Rektor said without turning his head one degree.

"Don't worry, Hans hasn't yet finished on the causes of the extinction of the earth worm."

"Good."

"Nervous?" Hidden under a blonde toupee, he whispered the one-word question with a kind smirk.

"Not particularly."

"No? If I were about to present to this audience what you claim to have obtained, I would be somewhat edgy, to say the least."

"Well… I—"

"Do you have the organisms?"

At that moment, Judith's face grew pale and adrenaline leapt up from her stomach.

"Yes." Without even thinking.

"Thank goodness." Altmann took a deep breath. "Five minutes until you're on. You won't have much time, so speak quickly. Try and take us up to sunrise, I want to avoid any foolish questions or objections."

"Sure," Judith backed away from the stage curtain,

"I just have to run to the bathroom."

Before the Rektor's objection reached her, she was around the corner of the hall and dashing down the emergency stairs. Upon making it to her car parked half on the curb, Judith looked straight past the luminous parking ticket taped to her windshield and swung open the back door to remove the forgotten wooden box.

//

Marc had just begun to dream when the history teacher pulled a cord that sent the white projector screen whizzing into the ceiling. The glare of the strong LEDs strained his eyes.

"Questions?" Through black-rimmed glasses the gangly teacher scoured the bored room, when a hand at the front darted up into the air.

"Why did our great-grandparents do this?" Came the naïve question from a front-row twit, followed by the laughter of the whole classroom.

"Quiet down, it's a perfectly good question... Well, put simply, they didn't know any better," the teacher revealed his wisdom in confidence.

"But the man in the film... he said there were warnings."

"That's correct, there were warnings. But not everybody listened to those warnings. You see, one must remember that our grandparents just weren't as wise as we are now, and they couldn't..." The teacher's monologue cut-off prematurely by the shrill ringing of the school bell, "You know what that means, children. You've got five minutes to grab a snack then head outside for sunrise."

Marc took his oversized rucksack from the cloakroom and escaped into the hallway before the rush. Completely oblivious to the fact that his hysterical mother was again breaking the twenty-five kilometre per hour speed limit in town and approaching the school in a panic, he slid from his bag the small wooden box that he had snatched confidently in one swift action from the back seat. Perching himself around a quiet corner and gazing at the box sitting softly in his hands, Marc's mind wondered as to what was so important that it had whipped his mother up into such frenzy earlier that morning. The boy's stare fixed, unable to look away; something inside radiated and caught his eye.

"Everybody please report to their designated areas," the silky voice of a custodian commanded through the loudspeakers. The ten year-old snapped to and stood. After checking down the hallway, he began making his way to the fire exit in large strides, holding his curious prize in front of his chest.

//

Tearing down the cobbled streets, Judith was no more than eight-hundred metres from her son, cursing herself for leaving that box anywhere near him. Cutting narrowly around the last corner, she came to a jolting stop as dozens of people marched over a street crossing and towards the car park on the other side of the street—'Zone 7'.

"Three minutes to sunrise. Everybody please report to their designated areas," the voice reverberated over and over again through the town.

"Come on! Move!" Judith yelled, with her fist shoved into the horn button. "Let's go!"

//

His thoughts meandering, Marc failed to notice the two pale twin girls in white dresses that had stepped out in front of him, centre of the corridor, linked arm in arm.

They too were skipping out on sunrise today. Holding out their hands and speaking in unison, they demanded the boy, considerably shorter than them, had to pay a toll in order to pass.

"I don't have any money."

"Too bad."

Marc knew he couldn't afford to waste time, the sun would be up in—

"Two minutes to sunrise. Everybody please report to their designated areas immediately," the voice this time was not so silky.

"I have something else." Marc had no other choice.

"What would that be?" The sceptical eleven year-old twins huffed together.

//

"Jesus Christ, please!" A kindergarten class was now sauntering over the same zebra crossing Judith had been held up at for the last two minutes. She was revving her engine at the five year-olds holding hands, dancing across the lines and jumping from white stripe to white stripe. But just as Judith gave in and let her heavy head fall flat onto the steering wheel, the road cleared almost instantly and she was off. "I might just make it," she thought. She hoped. Prayed.

"One minute to sunrise. Anybody not in their designated area wearing their UV-protection goggles will be fined. One minute to sunrise. Anybody not…"

Marc and his two followers galloped across the tall green grass towards the far corner of the school field so as not to get caught, filled with unknown adventure and a buzz like nothing before. Marc didn't quite know why.

The whole town gathered in the marked-out zones with their goggles fixed to their face like exemplary citizens, all staring in the same direction into the sky, waiting with grins on their faces for that roaring sphere of plasma to expose itself and bear its gift.

"Twenty seconds to sunrise. Please stand patiently." The last passage of the recording played, quieter than the rest. Then everything went silent.

//

Judith curbed her ride outside the front gates of the school and ran to the front of the closed building. The doors didn't slide open. The receptionist was with the rest, outside, counting down from five in her head. Throwing her whole body against the glass in a bid to break in, Judith would've looked like a desperate institute escapee to anyone that was watching. Nobody was.

//

Sitting tranquil in the itchy grass, the three children looked at the box without the tiniest comprehension of the consequences tied to what they were about to do.

"What now?" one of the girls whispered.

"Open it," the other egged Marc on.

Marc put his dirty right hand on the lid and his left on the base of the box, before, without question, without consideration, and allowing absolute curiosity to take charge of his choice, he slid open the top.

//

Judith sat hollow in her car, reconciling the fact that the last fifteen years of her career were possibly wasted. Almost half of her life spent searching, designing, testing, willing. All of those failed breeding programs, all of those colleagues that tried to convince her to quit, all of the bad press, the ethical questions. But what worried her most, what was eating at her core, the thought that was her fuel through everything that brought her to this point, was the question, what about the children?

//

The sun bleached lid lay discarded in the stinging nettles some metres from where the children sat, peering in, tightly huddled together, glaring over the box. Not a moment later, all three tilted their heads up in unison and embraced the sun with their faces. They watched as two vibrating black and gold honeybees, fuelled with the scent of freedom, emerged from the dark of the small wooden box and darted together vertically towards the patchy, temporarily-blue sky.

Shortly after their release, the children maintained faces of awe despite having lost track of the insects amongst the floaters clouding their vision; the two bees flitted in opposite directions, alone, as unconscious as the children of their own significance.

LR

Focus on ePublishing

#apocalypsepunkNOW

The London Reader

// INTRO // *While electronic reading was once heralded as the death of long-form writing, novel readership has grown in recent years thanks in part to self-published ebooks. Ike Hamill is a best-selling science fiction author on Amazon's Kindle. His excerpt included below gives us a quick look into the mainstream offshoot of the cyberpunk genre today. Following the popularity of television shows like The Walking Dead, he uses an apocalyptic setting but includes the shadows of authoritarian societies that the protagonists must still evade in the style of the cyberpunk genre. I have playfully called this genre #apocalypsepunkNOW.*

// This short excerpt from his Hamill's novella Madelyn's Confession, a part of his Madelyn Series, features survivors in a collapsing North America that has been wrecked by the consequences of insatiable greed. Hamill's stories can be read as survival-horror escapism. But while the setting may seem far-fetched, there's a certain masochistic glee in reading it as cyber-fairytale reflections of the recent political chaos on both sides of the Atlantic. In the excerpt, there are haunting echoes of the growing wealth divide and caustic current political climate in the United States as well as the ongoing refugee humanitarian crisis in the Mediterranean.

Madelyn's Confession

an excerpt from the novella

#apocalypsepunkNOW #excerpt

Ike Hamill

// BIO // *Ike Hamill writes fast-paced horror novels with strong, relatable characters. Since 2011 his books have gained a steady following amongst readers who enjoy his blend of sci-fi, paranormal, occult, and suspense. Hamill has written over 20 novels. Hamill cites Stephen King as one of his biggest influences. In his science fiction writing he prefers to portray a world that mirrors our own and then to twist it. His website is* **ikehamill.com**

BEFORE I LEFT the banks of Huron and skirted north to Lake Superior, I decided that I wanted to see the water one more time. I found a place where my train tracks got relatively close, and I set off south, through the trees. As night fell, I made a small fire on the bank of the river.

It was almost like camping.

The sky above was an endless ocean of black.

In the south, the clouds were lit up with orange from the city.

I heard them before I saw their lights. When they were still a hundred meters out, people wailed and screamed as the boat capsized. I threw all the wood I could find on the fire to make it a beacon for the swimmers. As they splashed and paddled towards me, I packed up my gear and retreated to the safety of the woods. I still wasn't sure what they were.

They dragged themselves up from the water, coughing and vomiting. They huddled around my fire for warmth. There were more than a dozen gathered there before the splashing stopped. They were all too exhausted and weak to be dangerous, but I kept my distance until one of them called to me.

"Hello?" a woman asked. Her voice was so pitiful. She hugged a little boy to her side and stroked his head.

"Who are you talking to?" someone asked.

"I saw a ghost in the trees," the woman said.

At the mention of a possible ghost, one of kids started to cry. I felt guilty that I was adding to their misery. I came into the circle of light from the fire.

"I'm not a ghost," I said. "That's my fire. Don't come closer. I'm armed."

"Who are you?" the woman with the little boy asked.

"Just a traveller."

"Thank you for building the fire. We couldn't see the shore," the woman said. "When the boat started to go down, I thought we would all drown," she said.

"Some did, thanks to you," a man croaked. He sounded miserable.

"I did what I had to do," the woman spat.

"Where did you come from?" I asked.

The woman glanced at the others and saw that nobody else was going to answer.

"We're from Bay City," she said. "It's north of Saginaw."

"I know it," I said. The place wasn't more than two-hundred kilometres north of Detroit.

"We had to get on the boat. There was nowhere else to go," she said. "The blast came up from Detroit, and the Buzzers came down from the Yoop. Death was all around us."

A guy from the other side of the fire interrupted before I could ask what she was talking about.

"Shut up," he said. "He's about to say something."

He leaned over the log next to him.

As the others gathered around, I realized that it wasn't a log. They were leaning in close to listen to a torso. It was burned so badly that it looked like a charred log. The arms and legs were gone. The mouth was a cracked red hole.

"What is he saying?" someone asked.

The man closest to the stump-man translated the whispers. "He says that it's not safe here. He says that the Buzzers are from this side of the lake and they hunt fire at night."

"What good has his advice done us?" a woman asked.

I was still standing several meters from the group. It seemed like maybe it was time for me to back away. I didn't want to know why they were dragging around a burned stump of a man and listening to him whisper.

"Shhh!" someone said.

All the heads turned towards the woods when we heard the click.

As weak and weary as they were, they gathered themselves together in an instant. Everyone began to splash back into the water. As I heard the second click, my mouth was hanging open. I couldn't believe that these people who had nearly drowned a moment before were now rushing back into the lake to stand with only their heads exposed. Even the kids were perfectly silent. Their wide eyes reflected back the firelight as they stared towards the woods.

Click.

Click.

My heart stopped as the noise in the woods took form.

LR

Upcoming Volumes

IF YOU enjoyed this volume of the London Reader, consider leaving a review on Goodreads or the Amazon storefront. Your comments will help bring readers and writers together through the pages of of upcoming volumes, like...

- Into the Eurozone & Onboard the Eurorail: Travel Stories from Beyond the Borders of Brexit
- South Asian Stories: Writing and poetry from India and beyond
- Grief & Loss: Stories of those loved and gone
- Altered States: Tales from beyond the edge of legalisation

Each volume of the London Reader is first released as a new issue for print and digital subscribers. If you don't want to miss a single issue of the London Reader, consider subscribing...

- to the Kindle edition in the UK: **www.amzn.to/2fvO7Th**
- to the Kindle edition in the US: **www.amzn.to/2gDSdG6**
- to the print or pdf edition anywhere in the world: **www.patreon.com/LondonReader**

LR

Free London Reader eBook

WANT A FREE digital copy of another volume of the London Reader? Join our mailing list to receive notifications of upcoming releases and receive a free edition of the London Reader in both print-replica pdf and easy-reading epub formats. Go to...

www.LondonReader.uk/Free

You will receive a free download of a recent volume of the London Reader in both pdf and epub versions, and you will be notified when future editions become available!

LR

Other Volumes

www.LondonReader.uk/Volumes

Cyberpunk in 2020
Science Fiction from Dystopian Moment to Sustainable Future

It's 2020—now where's my flying car?

Pat Cadigan famously answered, "That's not the future we promised you. We promised you a dark technological dystopia. How do you like it?" It's 2020, and the dark technological dystopia has arrived.

The fiction in this volume takes a look at the dystopian state of the world and dares to imagine an optimistic alternative. Will we continue down this path to self destruction, or do we dare envision a better future?

Cyberpunk in 2020 features a collection of multi-award-winning authors who move the genre away from the 80s action movie aesthetic of bakelite guns and neon-lit streets and into our increasingly networked existence facing ecological collapse. Stories from Nebula Award-winning authors Ken Liu, James Patrick Kelly, and Cat Rambo and from Arthur C Clarke Award-winners Gwyneth Jones and Lauren Beukes shine the light of their screens on this dark moment. This volume also interviews Pat Cadigan and the novelist and principal writer for Cyberpunk 2077, Jakub Szamalek.

These stories bring us up to date from the cyberpunk of the past. They attempt to debug the interconnected nature of the internet-driven world. They spring from our fears of climate catastrophe while at the same time offer us an alternative vision. The future the cyberpunk authors of the 80s warned us of is here. The dark technological dystopia is only getting worse. But it's not too late; there is still hope. The choice is ours.

Read the issue: **www.LondonReader.uk/Cyberpunk2020**

the LONDON READER
Autumn 2020
Contemporary Voices in Creative Writing

CYBERPUNK IN 2020

// FICTION BY
Gwyneth Jones
Lauren Beukes
and Ken Liu

// INTERVIEWS WITH
Pat Cadigan
and Jakub Szamalek of Cyberpunk

SCIENCE FICTION from DYSTOPIAN MOMENT to SUSTAINABLE FUTURE
James Patrick Kelly · Syd Shaw · Anthony Lapwood · Katie Harrison
Rosaleen Lynch · Rebecca Lee · Cat Rambo · Paige Elizabeth Wajda
Matt Bryden · Sergey Osipov · Pavlo Basandin · Janusz Orzechowski

After the Flood
Stories and Poems for our Changing World

the LONDON READER

Summer 2019

Contemporary Voices in Creative Writing

AFTER THE FLOOD

Stories and Poems for our Changing World

Featuring
ELLE WILD
OMAR EL AKKAD and
KIM STANLEY ROBINSON

David Ambarzumjan, Ivy Archer, Janette Ayachi, Steve Carr, Jill Evans
Matthew Gwethmey, Ira Joel Haber, AM Hayward, Katherine McMahon
Alice Mills, Artem Mirolevich, Robbi Nester, Claire Price, Christina Riley
Bell Selkie, Kai Thomas, Memye Curtis Tucker, Colleen West, Hannah Wright

TIDES RECLAIM coastal cities, forest fires choke the sky, heat waves scorch the plains, and in the eye of this catastrophe are the stories of families and communities—of fear and hope. The world faces a crisis, and we must search our souls for answers.

How can climate change fit into our stories? This issue of the London Reader re-maps the Earth with new and alternative visions of the present and the future. Stories and Poems for our Changing World faces crisis head-on, but the authors within come to many different conclusions. The cli-fi creative writing in this issue begins with pessimism, revealing the extent of natural disasters. It then revisits and re-evaluates our connection to the natural world. Finally, it finds a path forward, through calamity, with renewed ambition to make a difference.

After the Flood features an interview and fiction from Kim Stanley Robinson, the award-winning author of New York 2140 and the Mars Trilogy. The other creative works within include thought-provoking short stories from Elle Wild, Steve Carr, Hannah Wright, Kai Thomas, Katherine McMahon, Bell Selkie, and Omar El Akkad, author of American War; moving poems from Memye Curtis Tucker, Janette Ayachi, Ivy Archer, Colleen West, Matthew Gwathmey, Alice Mills, Robbi Nester, and Jill Evans; and stunning artwork from Artem Mirolevich, Christina Riley, Claire Price, David Ambarzumjan, and Ira Joel Haber, featured in the MoMA and Guggenheim.

We face a flood of unprecedented destruction. What will come after is up to us.

Read the issue now: **www.LondonReader.uk/AftertheFlood**

Drama & Dragons
Stories about Games and Growing up

the
LONDON READER
Autumn 2018
Contemporary Voices in Creative Writing

Drama & Dragons
Stories about Games and Growing up

Interviews with
Dragonlance author
Margaret
Weis
and the founders of
LitRPG
Vasily Mahanenko,
Alex Bobl, & D Rus

Introduced by
Steve Jackson
& Emily
Care Boss

Short Fiction by
Jeff Noon
Bridget Penney
& PK Merlott

Fantasy Gaming Fiction, Poetry, and Art by
Rachael Arsenault, Inbal Breda, Paul Carrick, Jesse Gazic, Holly Jennings,
Christine King, Ember Lane, Nicolò Maioli, Ian McLachlan, Kevin Oberlin,
d'Ores&Deja, Stefan Poag, Eric Quigley, Innes Smith, and more

FROM THEIR HUMBLE beginnings a half century ago, pen-and-paper roleplaying games like Dungeons & Dragons have gone on to become a global cultural phenomenon and inspired many generations of writers to think deeper about the stories they create. This issue of the London Reader delves into the worlds of these games and the stories of the people who play them.

Guest introductions by Emily Care Boss and Steve Jackson give insight into the connections between games and literature. Short stories, poetry, and art by Jeff Noon, author of Vurt; Bridget Penney; PK Merlott; Innes Smith; Jesse Gazic; Christine King; Rachael Arsenault; Ian McLachlan; d'Ores&Deja; Kevin Oberlin; Paul Carrick; Inbal Breda; Stefan Poag; Eric Quigley; and Nicolò Maioli all explore roleplaying games and the lives of their players. This issue also presents an interview with the New York Times best-selling author of the Dragonlance series, Margaret Weis.

Drama & Dragons includes a Bonus Feature with three one-page, ready-to-play roleplaying games that walk the line between literature and games, as well as a Bonus Feature on LitRPG fiction, a new genre of fantasy and sci-fi, where the stories take place within a computer game and the rules of the game impact the characters. This bonus section includes interviews with the founders of LitRPG as well as excerpts from LitRPG novels by Holly Jennings and Ember Lane.

Read the issue: www.LondonReader.uk/DramaAndDragons

Divisions
Stories of Inequality, Poverty, and Struggle

the
LONDON READER
Spring 2020
Contemporary Voices in Creative Writing

Divisions
Stories of Inequality,
Poverty, and Struggle

Featuring Fiction, Nonfiction, Poetry, and Art by
Tanatsei Gambura · Guy Prevost · Megan Carlson · Amy B Moreno
Rosa Borreale · Emily Rose Cole · Kevin Doyle · Susan G Duncan
PE Campbell · Kevin Fullerton · Leticia Mandragora · Delwar Hussain
Avra Margariti · Sorrah Edwards-Thro · Leo Wijnhoven · and George F

T HE 20s have returned with a roar. Wage inequality in the west is at its highest point since the Great Depression, and another global recession looms before many communities have even recovered from the last. What does it mean for those still struggling to thrive—or even just to survive? How do we criticise our own circumstances when it seems like someone else is always worse off? What causes the day-to-day struggles that define inequality in our lives? The answers are not so straightforward, but the pulse of the present moment can be found in its stories.

This collection brings together the beautiful and poignant stories, recollections, poems, and art of Tanatsei Gambura, Guy Prevost, Megan Carlson, Amy B Moreno, Rosa Borreale, Emily Rose Cole, Kevin Doyle, Susan G Duncan, PE Campbell, Kevin Fullerton, Leticia Mandragora, Delwar Hussain, Avra Margariti, Sorrah Edwards-Thro, Leo Wijnhoven, and George F.

What do they tell us about inequality and struggle? They say it is here, right here, as two people discuss an acquaintance's health concerns at brunch. They say, look, it followed us from the past when forty orphans arrived in Arizona by train. They say, we can feel it, right now, when pulling tight a blanket against the indoor cold. They say it is ongo-ing, and it is threatening to get worse. The creative writing in this issue doesn't have solutions, but it does have perspective, and we cannot change course until we know what course we are on.

Read the issue now: **www.LondonReader.uk/Divisions**

Other Volumes

#cyberpunkNOW
and the Dystopian Moment

Home: Stories of Identity
Belonging, Loss, and Migration

Love 2.0: Rewriting Romance
in the Digital Age

The Hate Speech Monologues

Other Volumes

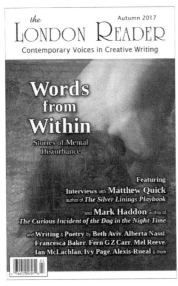

Words from Within:
Stories of Mental Disturbance

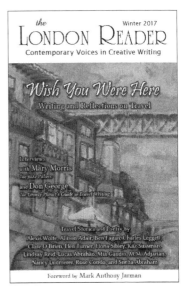

Wish You Were Here: Writing and
Reflections on Travel

After Words:
Animal Reflections

Truth, Lies, & Fiction
for a Post-Fact Age

Other Volumes

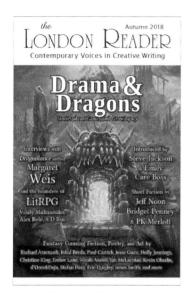

Drama & Dragons:
Stories about Games and Growing up

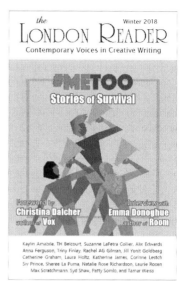

#MeToo:
Stories of Survival

Down & Out in Time & Space:
Stories and Poems of Time Travel

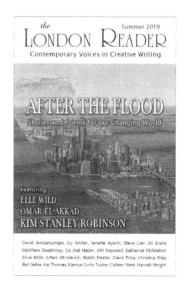

After the Flood: Stories and Poems
for our Changing World

Other Volumes

Existential Dread in the Digital Void:
Ominous Horror Stories

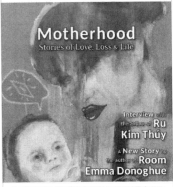

Motherhood:
Stories of Love, Loss, & Life

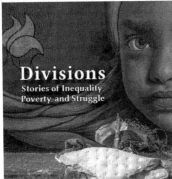

Divisions: Stories of Inequality
Poverty and Struggle

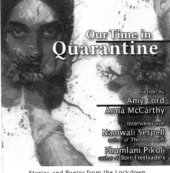

Our Time in Quarantine: Stories and
Poetry from the Lockdown

Print Subscriptions

Subscribe on Patreon.com

W E HOPE you've enjoyed reading this volume of the London Reader. If you would like to further support the contributors and collaborators of the London Reader, or if you'd like a new, **book-bound print issue** of the London Reader mailed directly to you with each new release, think about becoming a **Premium Print Subscriber** through the Patreon storefront.

For £9.99 ($13.99 US) per issue you receive...

- A new book-bound **print issue** of the London Reader four times per year.
- A **digital copy** of each new issue in pdf format.
- Access to subscriber-only **preview content** online.
- And you will be supporting the contributors and collaborators, allowing them to continue producing the writing that you love to read.

Become a print subscriber today. Visit **www.patreon.com/LondonReader** to subscribe!

LR

Printed in Great Britain
by Amazon